WOLF'S BABY

CODE OF THE ALPHA

LOLA GABRIEL

Wolf's Baby

Text Copyright © 2018 by Lola Gabriel

All rights reserved. This book or any portion thereof may not be reproduced or used in any manner whatsoever without the express written permission of the publisher except for the use of brief quotations in a book review.

This book is a work of fiction. Names, characters, places and incidents are either the product of the author's imagination or are used fictionally. Any resemblance to actual persons, living or dead, or to actual events or locales is entirely coincidental.

First printing, 2018

Publisher

Secret Woods Books
secretwoodsbooks@gmail.com
www.SecretWoodsBooks.com

PROLOGUE

The Splitting of the Pack

June 18, 1951
Silver Bay, Minnesota

THE CRESCENT MOON illuminated the dark velvet sky, accompanied by an array of stars, flickering at its brilliance. Its light cast a delicate shadow on the wooden two-story house nestled on a hill on the outskirts of Silver Bay. The Wylde family had decided to settle at the old farm due to the tranquility offered by the secluded area, the gentle running of the stream the only sound to interrupt the quietness and solace.

The Wyldes were a very private family, interacting solely with other wolves from their pack, and more often than not, they liked to spend their nights indoors.

That night, however, the tranquility was shattered by a

ruckus inside the basement. Luther Wylde, the head of the household and father to the five Wylde boys, had had enough.

"Silence!" A deep growl escaped from his throat and echoed along the walls of the basement. Within an instant, his five sons were quiet. They stood straight and still, knowing that their father was to be obeyed at all times. "I have made my decision."

The eldest of his sons, Cole, stepped forward. "Father, if I may?" he asked, and he only spoke again once his father nodded. "We have spent many nights arguing and stating our cases to you—" Disapproval laced through his voice as he briefly glanced at his brothers. "We still feel slightly—"

"Ignored, Father," Scout finished for Cole.

Luther narrowed his eyes. "Is that so?"

"What Scout is trying to say, Father," Kodiak said, taking a step forward, "is that we are a family, a unit. We need to stand together. We need to fight this! We cannot spend the rest of our lives running!"

"My decision is final," Luther told his sons. He turned to his wife, Skye, who stood next to him, and she gave him a slight nod of her head. They had made this decision together, and all that was left to do now was convince their sons that the matter was settled.

"But they will find us," Kodiak continued, his voice urgent. "I've seen the way they look at us, Father, and they know what we are!"

River, the youngest of the Wylde boys, said in a quiet voice, "We should leave."

"We are *not* going anywhere," Luther growled, clenching his fists.

"You would sentence us to death?" Scout cried.

"Enough!" Luther snapped. "I will not have my sons defy my orders."

Wren, who had remained quiet throughout the entire argument, murmured, "They will come and kill us."

"No one is going to come and kill us," Skye said, raising her hands as if she were a moderator between her husband and her sons. "Not tonight, not ever."

"And that's the end of this discussion," Luther finished.

Kodiak gritted his teeth together. "Father—!"

It only took a scathing look from Luther for his sons to lower their glances to the ground. Without another word, they cleared out of the basement, heading up the stairwell to their respective rooms.

Skye approached Luther and gently placed a comforting hand on his shoulder. Neither of them wanted to have such a dispute with their sons, and their fear of being discovered was not misplaced. But their duty to protect their family and their pack came above anything else, and if that meant that they couldn't tell their children everything they knew, so be it.

RIVER WAS AWOKEN by the sound of Scout's heartbeat. His brother was awake and... alarmed. Why? Was something wrong? River couldn't hear anything out of the ordinary—everyone else in the house seemed to be asleep—so he climbed out of bed and headed to Scout's room. Perhaps his brother had simply had a bad dream, or maybe he was thinking about their earlier conversation with Father, and River was worrying over nothing.

He'd rather be safe than sorry, though.

River's room was in the middle of the hallway, right in front of the staircase leading down. To his right were Scout's and Wren's rooms, while Cole's and Kodiak's were on his left. He walked past Wren's door, and he smiled softly when he heard his brother's light snoring.

Once he was standing in front of the open doorway of

Scout's room, he knocked on the door to announce his presence.

"Scout?" River asked. Scout was at the window, seemingly glancing through it at something that had his posture rigid. "Is everything okay?"

His brother didn't answer him.

"Scout?" he called again, finally catching Scout's attention. River rubbed the drowsiness off his eyes. "What's going on?"

Scout's eyes were wide, and River was about to repeat the question when his brother spoke. "Do you hear anything?"

Before River could even ask what Scout was talking about, a distant sound he couldn't identify echoed in his ears. The closer it sounded, the more River could start figuring out what it was. After a few seconds, the source of the noise was almost as clear as if River saw it in front of his eyes.

"Footsteps," he whispered anxiously. "It... it sounds like half the town is coming." Perhaps it was a hyperbole, but the words hadn't felt like such an exaggeration to him.

"Go get Cole and Kodiak," Scout told him, moving to the door. "Get them and tell them we need to get out of—!"

His sentence was cut short by something crashing through the window, shattering the glass all across the floor of Scout's room. River couldn't see exactly what it was; all he saw was an object on fire—possible a torch—setting the wooden floorboards underneath him and Scout ablaze.

"*Go!*" Scout yelled at him, and River rushed out of the room and toward his brothers'. He could feel the flames trailing behind him, almost licking at his ankles, and he sped up his pace.

"Kodiak!" River screamed, briefly stopping at Kodiak's door to make sure that he woke at the sound of his voice before rushing to Cole's room, which was at the end of the hallway. Cole was already groggily getting out of bed, rubbing the back of his neck. "Cole! Cole, we have to go!"

Wolf's Baby 5

Cole, with his eyes half-closed, stumbled to the doorway. "What are you talking—?" He glimpsed at the fire raging behind River, his sentence cutting off as he grabbed River's shoulder and pushed him along the hallway and towards the staircase. Kodiak was already halfway down the stairs, and he glanced at the other side of the hallway, which was almost entirely engulfed in flames now.

"Wren!" River cried. "Scout!"

"Wren's trapped in his room!" Scout yelled from somewhere amidst the inferno, but the flames were too big for River to see him. "I need to get him out!"

"You *both* need to get out here *now*!" Kodiak screamed, yelping when the banister of the staircase began to catch on fire, crumbling before him.

Cole gripped River's arms and looked straight into his eyes. "River, you and Kodiak need to go."

"What? No!" River argued, vehemently shaking his head. "What about you and Scout and Wren?"

"I have to make sure they find a way out of those flames," Cole said, his voice stern and determined. "And I have to look for Mother and Father."

"But—"

Cole reassuringly squeezed his arms. "We'll be right there, okay? I promise."

Although River wanted to stay to help his brothers, he knew he would only become a nuisance to their survival. If they had any hopes of getting out of the house before it burned down around them, he had to get out with Kodiak. He nodded at Cole, who smiled at him and then turned towards the fire, seemingly bracing himself to run into it.

"The window!" Cole screamed to the flames, holding his arms in front of him. Then he jumped back into the inferno, and River had to restrain himself from going after him.

He glanced at the staircase, its banisters already crumbling to ashes, the floorboards underneath River about to follow suit. Kodiak was at the bottom of the stairs, holding his arms out.

"Come on, little brother!" he exclaimed. "I won't let you fall!"

Before he could think about it, River ran to the beginning of the blazing staircase, closed his eyes, and leaped off the ground as it gave way underneath him.

Kodiak, true to his word, caught him in his arms, and the two of them rushed out of the house and away from the escalating fire.

THEY FOUND WREN, Scout, and Cole laying in a grassy ditch down the hill from their house, coughing their lungs out and gasping for air, their faces streaked with ash and smoke. River assumed they had jumped out of a window, though he didn't particularly care for how his brothers had gotten out. All that mattered was that they had.

"You're okay!" he cried, lunging at them and doing his best to wrap his arms around all three of them.

"Barely," Wren joked, and River laughed, tears welling up in his eyes.

"Wait," said Kodiak, standing behind him. "Where... where are Mother and Father?"

River felt Cole tense in his embrace, and he pulled apart to look at the eldest of his brothers. "Cole?" he asked tentatively. "Where are Mother and Father? You... you said you were going to look for them, where"

Wren and Scout stared at the grass beneath them, and Cole slowly shook his head.

"River, listen—" he started to say.

"No," River mumbled, the tears in his eyes spilling down his face. "No."

"River—"

"*No!*" River yelled. He turned to their burning house on the hill and started to run towards it, but he was caught in the arms of one of his brothers. "Let me go! We have to get them!"

"You can't go back there!" Scout shouted. Was he the one holding River in place?

"We *have* to!" River snapped, desperately struggling against Scout's grip. "We have to get Mother and Father!"

"There's nothing left, River!" Scout screamed. "Look, River! It's all gone!"

River stared at the old farm that was... that had *been* his home, his family's home, for longer than any other place had been. He focused on his mother's heartbeat, his father's breathing, any sound that would tell him that they were okay, that his parents had made it out before them, that... that they weren't—

He couldn't hear anything beyond the raging fire engulfing his home, burning it down to the ground.

"I don't see them, River," Scout mumbled hoarsely, his grip lessening so much that River crumbled to his knees, unable to hold himself up without his brother. "I... I don't see anything."

River picked up all the noises around him, even if all he wanted was to ignore them: the sound of Kodiak gritting his teeth in anger; the sound of Wren running his fingers through his hair and holding his head, muttering under his breath; the sound of Cole's breathing, calm and collected even as he shook with fury; the sound of footsteps approaching...

The sound of footsteps approaching.

"We have to go," River mumbled, his eyes widening even though he continued to stare at the building engulfed in flames on the hill. "I hear them coming this way."

Despite knowing they couldn't remain where they were, River couldn't stand up. He felt someone hoisting him up by the collar of his shirt, and his legs started cooperating enough for him to follow his brothers into the marsh, where they found a hiding spot between the overgrown weeds.

River felt like they stayed there for an eternity. All of them were quiet, doing their best to keep their breathing as quiet as they could—except for Wren, who had to cover his mouth as tears spilled from his eyes, hushed, muffled sobs escaping his lips every few seconds. Finally, Scout heaved a sigh and whispered, "They're gone."

The five of them sat at the edge of the bank and stared morosely at the fiery remnants of their home. Neither of them said a word for what felt like too long.

"What are we supposed to do now?" River asked once he couldn't deal with the silence anymore. He assumed, by the looks of his brothers' faces, that the general consensus of what the answer would be was, *I don't know*.

But then Cole took a deep breath and said, "We have to split up."

"*What*?" the rest of them cried in unison.

"That's the last thing Father would want us to do!" River exclaimed, heartbroken at the mere suggestion of tearing their family apart even further.

"As the eldest," Cole said, glancing at him with eyes that shone with anger, "I think I'm the only one who should make a decision like this, and I say we split up."

"You can't make that call by yourself!" Scout replied, getting up to his feet. "This affects all of us, Cole. We should all have a say in what we do now!"

"Do you have any other idea, Scout?" Cole growled, standing up to look down at his brother. "Because unless you do, splitting up is our only choice!"

"Can you *please* calm down?" River demanded, standing between his arguing brothers. Couldn't they see they didn't have

Wolf's Baby

9

time to fight amongst themselves? Couldn't they see now was the time to stay together and stand by each other's side?

"Stay out of this, River," Cole snarled, his gaze still focused on Scout. "This doesn't concern you."

"Oh, what," River replied, "you think that just because I'm the youngest that I don't matter!"

"I told you to stay out of this!" Cole repeated, glaring at River.

"You're not the alpha!" River yelled, all of his pain and heartbreak and the loss and grief he hadn't allowed himself to feel just yet bursting out right alongside his words.

"River—" Wren tried to say, but River was undeterred.

"You think you get to make the decisions now? You think you're better than us? Stronger, more powerful, more entitled, just because you're the eldest? Guess what, Cole— your birthright means *nothing* now! We just lost our parents, and all you can think about is how to break this family apart even more! You want to be the alpha so badly? Be my guest!"

Without giving his brother a chance to respond, River turned around and walked toward the woods, fuming with every step he took.

"River!" Kodiak called him. "River, come on, what—what are you doing? Where are you going?"

"Following his orders! I'm splitting up!" River shouted over his shoulder. "I'm getting as far away from Cole as possible!"

"River!" he heard Wren scream. Scout also cried out his name, telling him to come back, they could work this out... but River was done. He kept walking, his legs carrying him deeper into the woods, listening to his brothers argue amongst themselves.

He kept walking, even as their voices started fading away one by one, each of them leaving Cole alone in the marsh.

He kept walking until he couldn't hear any of them anymore.

1

Coleman, Wisconsin

THE WISCONSIN SKY was cold and fresh as the darkness settled in a heavy blanket over the rolling hills, particularly in the small Midwestern town of Coleman, Wisconsin. The tree branches and ground were covered in a thick layer of winter snow, as they usually were this time of year. It was long past midnight and the town slumbered peacefully, unaware of the fear and anxiety that was about to boil up inside a house on Elm Drive.

Liya Channing opened her eyes as a powerful stabbing pain ripped through her skull, and the world swam around her. She slowly pushed herself up from the cold floor of her bathroom and felt the tightness of her scalp ease slightly. It had been yet another torturous and anger-filled night for Liya. She scrambled to her feet, and almost didn't recognize the person in the mirror. She wasn't even five hundred years old, but she felt much older, especially after what had happened tonight. Her blonde hair hung lifelessly around her narrow shoulders and her blue eyes

—which were once filled with light and hope—were now two dark pools of sorrow and nothingness.

Liya stepped out of the bathroom quietly and into the hallway. The floor was cold against the soles of her feet and as she approached the door at the end of the hallway, she stopped. Liya peeked inside and saw the silhouette of her daughter, Illa, sleeping soundly in her crib. She smiled sadly and stepped away from the door. She was quite surprised that the noise of her cries and his growls didn't wake Illa, but she was relieved as well.

Liya carefully walked back to her bedroom and was almost too afraid to enter the dark room, but to her relief, she realized the room was in fact empty. She sat down on the bed and bit her lower lip.

When she met Hunter Duncan four years ago, he was charming and easy to fall in love within such a short space of time. He was very attractive, with dark brown hair and bright blue eyes much like her own, only darker. They had met at a bar that Hunter frequented and, soon afterward, had moved in together. Liya was happy, and despite her parents' wishes to take things slow and be wary, she took that step.

Then things started to change for the worse, as they usually did.

Hunter became obsessed, as he was a hunter wolf, and soon his violent nature and short temper became apparent, leaving Liya terrified every minute of every day. Hunter apologized, of course, and promised that he would change, but he never did. When Liya told him that she was pregnant, things seemed to calm down. He was calmer, but his troubled demeanor always seemed to lurk beneath the surface. Hunter spent most of his nights out—at bars and clubs—while Liya stayed home with Illa.

A shiver ran down her spine as she thought of all the nights she spent fearing for her life as Hunter unleashed his temper on her. Luckily, he never touched Illa. Liya was not a violent person, but if any harm came to Illa, there would be hell to pay, and somehow she hoped that Hunter knew this.

She ran her fingers through her long, blonde hair and tied it up on top of her head. Her scalp ached again from the pressure and she cringed slightly. She had had enough. She couldn't go on like this any longer. Too many nights had she spent at the mercy of that cruel, vindictive man. Too many nights had she been pushed around and beaten on by that man. Too many nights had she woken up in a daze after that man threw her around. Too many nights had she spent on the floor wishing she was dead. She couldn't take it any longer. There was no use fighting back—Hunter was just too strong, and she definitely didn't want to leave Illa at the mercy of her father.

Liya's hands started to shake from all the anger inside her, but she simply stared at them. She was paralyzed with fear, but she also knew that she needed to do something. She would eventually die at the hands of Hunter, that much she knew. She stood up shakily and glanced around her. She crouched down in front of the bed, her body aching from the damage done by a man who claimed to love her, a man with whom she'd had a child, a man who didn't deserve her, or Illa, for that matter.

She slid a large suitcase out from under the bed and emptied her drawers and her closet into it. Not everything was going to fit, so she only took the essentials. She loaded her suitcase into the car and went back upstairs to pack Illa's things. She packed everything into the car before carefully scooping Illa up in her arms and taking her outside. She gently placed her in her car seat, in its reclining position, buckled her in and covered her little body with a fluffy blanket. Liya placed her baby bag with all her essentials—such as bottles and diapers—on the back seat and closed the door of the car. She pulled the car out onto the driveway and locked it. She didn't like leaving Illa alone inside the car, but she couldn't take her along with what she had planned next.

Grabbing a full can of gas from the garage and walking with purpose through the house, the home she had built with Hunter, she poured the gasoline over the furniture. She made her way back to the garage and placed the now-empty gas can on the wooden bench. She took a few steps back, pulled her lighter from her jacket pocket and lit it. She took a few deep breaths before throwing it into the garage and then rushed to the car. She checked the back seat, where Illa slept, completely unaware of the turmoil around her.

Liya climbed into the car and slowly drove off, watching in the rearview mirror as the flames started to engulf the house, her old life.

It was time to leave this life behind for good, or it would be the end of her.

Liya didn't have a set destination, and simply drove. She drove until the sun came up, fueled by the desire to keep herself and her daughter safe. She also knew that Hunter would be able to track her if she knew in advance where she was going, so she simply kept driving. She just wanted to get as far away from Hunter and his pack as possible.

Hunter belonged to a massive pack, originating from Louisiana, but having branched out to the Midwest. Hunter was a Zeta and he was considered a valuable member due to his hunting abilities, which was also why his violent behavior was ignored, making Liya out to be a liar. The pack members simply turned a blind eye, and it was not something that they addressed.

Hunter could literally find a needle in a haystack and this was what made him both valuable and dangerous, especially to his enemies. Although, now thinking back, Liya felt she was in more danger than his enemies.

Wolf's Baby 15

Liya was passing through a small town in Minnesota called Easton when Illa started to make a fuss. Liya stopped at a gas station to fill up her car and she couldn't help but glance around her with paranoia. By now Hunter would be standing in front of their burnt-down home, ready to kill, and Liya didn't want to be anywhere near him when that happened.

"Hey, baby," Liya smiled and took Illa out of her seat. "Are you hungry, baby girl?"

Liya and Illa went for a quick breakfast at a diner across the street, which was quite nice for a small town. Illa had fun throwing the straws and napkins onto the floor, and although Liya apologized profusely to the waitress about the mess, the middle-aged waitress simply smiled, saying, "It's no problem. As long as she's having fun, right?"

Liya was grateful to the friendly waitress, and she felt a little more relaxed. She knew she couldn't keep driving too long with Illa in the car, as Illa loved moving around and detested staying in her car seat for long periods of time, but at this moment, Liya knew that she didn't have much of a choice.

As Liya and Illa headed back to her car, she noticed a police cruiser slowly drive past her and her heart started to pound in her chest. She wondered whether Hunter had involved the police or not, but knowing him, he'd take matters into his own hands.

Or his pack would.

She buckled Illa into her seat, giving her a fresh bottle, and just as she was about to close the door, she noticed the police cruiser stop a few yards from her. Her chest tightened as she closed the rear door and walked around to the driver's side door.

To her dismay, a police officer climbed out of the cruiser and approached her car.

This is it. I am so busted, she thought to herself as she climbed into the car, closing the door abruptly.

"Good morning, ma'am," the officer said in a strange accent she didn't recognize.

"Good morning, officer," she greeted him politely. "Is there a problem?"

"No, not at all. I noticed you're from Wisconsin," he answered and stopped in front of her window.

"Yes, that's right."

"You're a long way from home."

"My daughter and I are visiting family in Washington," she said nonchalantly, surprised at how easily she lied.

Desperate times called for desperate measures.

"Why didn't you just fly?" he asked. "Wouldn't that be easier with a baby?"

Liya narrowed her eyes for a moment and placed her hand on the steering wheel. As she was about to answer, she noticed the officer look at her hand and he suddenly began to back away. There was visible fear in his eyes and he held one of his hands up in the air.

"I'm sorry that I bothered you, ma'am. Have a safe journey," the officer said and turned on his heel, hurrying back to his cruiser.

Liya frowned, slightly confused for a moment, and glanced down at her hand. On her skin was a small tattoo in the shape of a crescent moon, which was exposed to the officer when she had placed her hand on the steering wheel.

The crescent moon tattoo was a symbol of Hunter's exclusive pack and it certainly had its benefits being a member. It struck fear into the eyes and hearts of even the most powerful Alphas in the country. The tattoo, or even the mention of the pack's name, was enough to command the utmost respect from anyone who saw or heard it.

The Crescents.

Wolf's Baby 17

Dating back to the 18th century, the Crescents settled in Louisiana, or more specifically, New Orleans. They were originally from France and had traveled to New Orleans a few years after it was founded. The packs settled into the lush plantations in the area, and they were much happier, free from the persecution that almost led to the extinction of the pack. They weren't the friendliest bunch, and in the mid-19th century, another pack threatened to take over their lands, but the Crescents' Alphas and Betas slaughtered the entire pack, burning their bodies in a pyre.

They were brutal and straight-up terrifying. Definitely not a pack to mess around with.

Although Liya didn't agree with the way the pack was run, she had very little say, as she was not born into the pack. When she met Hunter, he introduced her to the Delta and the Epsilons. Because she was his partner, or mate—even though they never actually imprinted—she was now a member by default. She never felt like a member, though, feeling more like an outsider during their entire relationship. Everything was on a need-to-know basis when it came to Hunter and the things he did for the pack. Liya was well aware that Hunter had so much blood on his hands that not even the ocean would be able to wash it off, and she wondered why she had become involved with him in the first place.

Still, having the tattoo was as beneficial as it was an inconvenience.

Liya started the car and drove off, not seeing the police cruiser anywhere.

After stopping at a hotel in North Dakota, and a few more stops along the way, Liya realized that she needed to figure out where she and Illa were headed. She was starting to get tired again, and Illa had begun to niggle in her car seat.

In the distance, she could make out the lights of a town, and as she drove closer, she noticed the sign on the side of the road just before entering the town.

"Bigfork, Montana," she said quietly and glanced in the rearview mirror at Illa, who was on the verge of having a meltdown in her seat. "How does that sound?"

Illa looked back at her with pleading eyes filled with tears and a pout on her lips.

"Okay, Bigfork it is, then," Liya said, feeling rather relieved that they were stopping for the night, hopefully for a while. She was tired and craved a hot bath and a comfortable bed.

She parked in front of a cozy motel and booked her and Illa a room for the night. She lugged their suitcases into their room then sunk wearily onto the bed to catch her breath for a moment. After they had a bath, Illa clambered around the room exploring her new surroundings, while Liya sat on the bed paging through the newspaper in search of a more permanent residence. Bigfork was as good a place as any, and best of all, it was not under the control of the Crescents.

Liya glanced over at Illa, who had toppled over the dustbin and now wore it as a hat, and chuckled. All Liya wanted was for Illa to grow up never knowing the fear and the pain that had become her way of life these last four years. She wanted her daughter to have a better future, even if that meant not knowing her father, but maybe it was better this way. No one needed an abusive person in their life, especially not at such a young age.

After Illa fell asleep on the bed, Liya continued to look through the newspaper before turning in for the night. She hadn't realized how exhausted she was until she rested her head on the pillow, falling asleep almost immediately.

WHEN LIYA OPENED her eyes the next morning, she was

Wolf's Baby 19

surprised to feel incredibly well rested, despite the ordeal that she had been through. She sat up in bed and stretched her arms above her head.

Liya glanced over at Illa, who lay smiling at the ceiling.

"Good morning, baby girl," Liya said with a smile. "How did you sleep? Was it fun?"

Illa giggled and chortled which made Liya smile even more. She rubbed her daughter's belly, and her tattoo caught her eye again, making her remember the expression on the police officer's face when he saw it and realized she was a Crescent. Was he a wolf as well, or had he encountered more than his fair share of Crescent members? This made Liya wonder whether she had made the right choice to drive in this direction. Were there many other Crescents in the area?

Then again, the police officer had an accent and probably only recently moved away from a Crescent-infested city or town. Besides, Minnesota was a long way from Montana.

Liya quickly got dressed and then changed Illa's diaper and clothes as well. They headed out to a nearby diner for breakfast, and then into town to buy herself a new phone. She and Illa went into the local real estate office and she spoke with Linda, a young agent.

To Liya's amazement, Linda showed her a lovely house close to Flathead Lake, surrounded by trees. Linda assured her that it was a safe area and the unit was even fully furnished. Liya loved it, especially the small porch that had an amazing view of the forested area behind the house, and as an added bonus, it was available immediately.

Because Liya and Illa had only their two suitcases, it didn't take long for them to move out of the motel and into the new place. Liya even opened a bank account into which she transferred all of her money, and she even took the money from the account she shared with Hunter. She was pretty sure that

Hunter would explode if he found that out, but she didn't care. No one was going to touch her in Bigfork.

She would make sure of that.

As she and Illa sat on the wooden bench on their new porch, watching the sunset, Liya finally felt at peace. She knew that it was because of Illa, because Illa was born with the ability to bring calm to any given situation—when she was awake. It didn't really matter whether it was self-procured or through her beautiful daughter, all she knew was that they were safe.

Even if it was for only a short while.

2

Bigfork, Montana

THE FIRE CAME CLOSER and Wren's chest tightened as the smell of burning flesh filled his nostrils. He heard his brothers shouting in the distance, but he couldn't see anything. The smoke was too thick and dense. A ringing sounded in his ears and his eyes burned from the heat. The feeling of helplessness filled him to the core, and as the searing heat cornered him, the flames licking at his feet, his body jolted upright. Panting in the darkness, the images in his head dissipated with the realization that it had been yet another dream.

When will this nightmare end? he wondered to himself as he tried to calm his beating heart. His entire body was covered in perspiration and it didn't surprise him. Today would have been his mother's birthday, although he had lost count as to how old she would have been. Of the five Wylde brothers, Wren was the one who was closest to their mother, Skye Wylde. Wren was born earlier than he was supposed to be, hence his mother was a little more protective of him. He was relentlessly teased as a child, and even as a teenager, for being a 'Momma's boy',

Even after their home was burnt down in Minnesota nearly sixty-seven years ago, Wren still had nightmares of that night. Of course, his nightmares were nothing close to what he had actually experienced, but he *did* have a tendency to exaggerate a little, being a Momma's boy and all—according to his oldest brother, Cole.

Even though Wren would give anything to find or see his four brothers again, he knew that too much time had passed and that his brothers would be nothing like how he remembered them. Wren didn't regret leaving, although he wished he had someone who was as close to him as a brother, but would never openly admit it to anyone. Luckily, he didn't have the opportunity to open up to anyone.

Being the Alpha of the Montana pack came with many pros, and not having to open up to people was one of them. Sure, it wasn't healthy to bottle up feelings, allowing them to fester, but losing his parents in a house fire, injuring his shoulder *and* losing his brothers because they didn't have the balls nor the tenacity to agree on *anything* in one night, weren't healthy either.

Wren sure as hell didn't dwell on the past and what could have been, but he also didn't feel sorry for himself so that others would notice. He was the Alpha, and he wasn't allowed to get emotional over anything. In fact, he had closed himself off to emotion so well, that he could banish a pack member without batting an eyelid. He didn't have the patience or the energy to deal with disloyalty and mutiny—he had endured an abundance of that in his lifetime.

His brothers, especially Cole, often accused him of having 'middle child syndrome', which he probably had, but he didn't want to hear about it, especially not from Cole.

Cole was an asshole, plain and simple. Everyone knew it,

even Cole. He thought that he alone should be the Alpha of his father's pack in Minnesota, not even giving the other four brothers a chance to state their case. Their father, Luther Wylde, was a strict man who followed the rules his entire life, and this infuriated the other younger brothers. Wren remembered the nights when Scout would run off into the mountains out of frustration, and would only return a few days later. Skye and Wren's older brother, Kodiak, had been the peacekeepers of the family, having the necessary emotional abilities. However, Scout's defiance and Cole's arrogance were not curable. To be honest, Wren wasn't sure if it was arrogance or sheer stupidity.

Wren climbed out of bed and shuffled through the house. The sun hadn't risen yet, and there was no way that Wren would be able to fall asleep again. The nightmare had felt so real this time around and he shivered as he thought about it. There was an eerie feel inside his home, yet there was no one there.

Wren's sense of smell was extraordinarily strong, and he could even smell if it was going to rain, in another state, in a week's time. He recognized the scent of every single member of his pack and immediately knew when there was a newcomer in town, whether it was temporary or permanent.

It was never permanent.

People didn't *willingly* move to Bigfork.

Sure, the scenery was beautiful, and the people were friendly most of the time, but after the flood of 1943, people avoided living in Bigfork. They would pass through, enjoy the scenery, and be on their merry way. Wintertime and the rainy season, which felt as if it was all the time, saw the least amount of visitors, which was fine by Wren. He hated newcomers, because they were nothing but trouble.

Wren opened the two large doors that led to the back porch and stepped onto the paving. Flathead Lake was sprawled out in front of him, its smooth surface appearing mirror-like, reflecting the moon and the stars clearly. To Wren it reminded him of the marsh behind their family home in Minnesota, and he often wondered when whoever burnt down that house would be coming for him.

It had occurred to him many times that his brothers may possibly be dead already, but it didn't matter. He couldn't look for them. He had enough on his plate as it was.

A sudden breeze picked up, and Wren caught a strange scent. He scowled as he shook his head in disapproval.

"Stupid humans," he muttered, but as he was about to walk back into the house, he froze.

That's not human, he thought to himself.

It was a wolf.

There was a new wolf in town.

SUTTON, Wren's Beta, glanced at him as they walked along the main road a few hours later. Sutton was the closest thing to a friend that Wren had, but that was where it ended. Wren knew that it was incredibly difficult for Sutton, or anyone, to get to know him well enough to know what he was thinking. Not even a mindreader could figure out what Wren was thinking—he was pretty skilled at closing himself off completely. He was a closed book and intended on keeping it that way. Sutton didn't even attempt to break through those impenetrable walls he had built, as it was only a waste of energy to try to get through them. Sutton had tried once too many times and it left him exhausted and even more frustrated than before.

Obviously, Wren had his reasons for being this way, and thankfully Sutton accepted that, because everyone had their own shit they had to deal with.

"What's going on, Wren?" Sutton asked and regarded him

with dark eyes. "We've been walking along the main road for almost an hour now. What are we looking for?"

"I told you. There's a newcomer in town, and I want to know who it is," Wren muttered, digging his hands into the front pockets of his brown leather jacket.

"So, what are you going to do when you find him?" Sutton asked.

"It all depends on why he's here, and..." Wren stopped suddenly and glanced through the window of the grocery store.

"Wren, are you okay?"

Wren nodded. "I'm fine. You should go take care of your patrols."

"I thought we were doing just that," Sutton answered.

Wren looked at him with a blank expression. Sutton had been a member of Wren's pack for a long time, so he should know that Wren always patrolled by himself. Wren gave new meaning to the term 'lone wolf' and everyone knew that about him. Even though he was often on his own, he was definitely not weak or vulnerable. In fact, Wren was at his strongest and most powerful when he was alone. He'd draw out his energy and power from nature, and even though he wasn't the tallest or brawniest Alpha in the country, he was strong and a force to be reckoned with. Some would say that he might appear a little heartless and cruel, but this was brought on by the cruelty he had endured.

"Fine, I'll just be on my way, then," Sutton said as he stepped away from Wren, but Wren was a little too preoccupied to answer him. The scent of the new wolf in town became stronger as Wren stepped closer to the shop window. Glancing through the glass he scanned the patrons inside, and a strange feeling rose up inside him. He wasn't sure what it was, but it soon vanished when he saw the owner of the store walk his way. The owner opened the door and glared at him with a furrowed brow.

"Can I help you with something?"

Wren cleared his throat and looked at the owner. "No, I just thought I saw someone I used to know a long time ago."

The owner, of course, wasn't a wolf, and Wren had no desire to make small talk with him, so he stepped off the sidewalk and proceeded back to his car, which was parked about five blocks away. Wren hadn't realized that he and Sutton had walked as far as they did, but it didn't really matter.

Wren reached his car and climbed inside. His red BMW roared to life and he pulled away abruptly. His father would definitely not approve of this car at all, since it stood out like a sore thumb. Wren was done with being inconspicuous and trying to remain undetected. Luckily, the townspeople of Bigfork were as discreet as they were backstabbing. Or maybe they were just too oblivious for their own good.

Wren secretly despised the humans. Not only because of their fragile nature and their inability to keep things to themselves, but also their smell.

There was something about a human that simply repulsed him. He recalled a few instances involving humans when he was young, and they still lived on their land in Minnesota. They especially stank in the summertime, which puzzled a young Wren, as they didn't have any fur, or maybe that was the reason. No fur to mask the odor. Because of his strong sense of smell, the ghastly aroma of sweaty humans swimming in the lakes or pools, or wherever they were swimming, repulsed Wren to the point where he had to lock himself in the basement while his brothers enjoyed the days of summer.

Of course, Wren didn't mind, as his mother would sit with him in the basement so that he wouldn't be alone. They talked about everything imaginable, and Wren considered himself the luckiest kid in the world to have a mother like the one he had.

And then she was gone, taken from him before he could

even tell her that he loved her one last time, or hug her, or feel her fingers raking through his hair when he was upset. He hoped that she knew how much she meant to him, but he would never know for sure.

He heard a sudden crash and his car suddenly jolted forward. "What the..." he muttered and glanced in his rearview mirror.

A light blue car had driven right into his rear bumper, and his jaw clenched in anger. He yanked his door open and climbed out of the car, ready to give whoever was behind the wheel a big piece of his mind. He was sure that he hadn't been too distracted on the road, or preoccupied with the memories of his mother, or the smell of the mysterious newcomer, so it must have been the other driver's fault. He marched to the other car just as a young woman with long blonde hair climbed out of the driver's seat.

"You just drove right into my car! Can't you watch the road?" he exclaimed angrily.

"I'm so sorry," she stuttered, and she glanced at him, her eyes red and filled with tears.

Wren stopped in his tracks and stood frozen on the spot. The tears in her eyes weren't solely due to the fact that she had just caused a huge amount of damage to Wren's rear bumper. Something was wrong, and Wren could feel it. He didn't have the emotional connection to others the way his mother and Kodiak had, but he could definitely sense that something was wrong.

The young woman, who was now sobbing almost uncontrollably, stood before him. "I am so sorry," she repeated between heaving sobs.

"Are you okay?" he asked as he walked closer to her. He felt bad for her, and he didn't understand why.

"No, I am not okay. I—I just ran into your car," she stammered and looked down at the ground. "Are *you* okay?"

"I'm fine. It's just a bumper," he answered calmly, which surprised him.

Under normal circumstances, he'd be livid, but there was something about this young woman who made the entire world slow down. The ringing in his ears was gone, and his mind felt completely clear.

She looked at him, her pale blue eyes brightening slightly as she gazed into his eyes. Her words, as well as her tears, stopped for a moment as they stared at one another.

Then, the moment was gone, and as she turned away slightly, he was left still wanting more. *She* was the wolf, the newcomer in town.

She was *the* wolf.

Wren held his hand out to her and said in a deep voice, "I'm Wren Wylde."

"Liya Channing," she said and shook his hand with reluctance before turning to gaze back at her car.

It was only then when he noticed the baby in the back seat, nonchalantly drinking from a bottle, completely unfazed about the drama that unfolded outside of the car.

"She's beautiful," Wren said without thinking.

"Thank you," she responded with a slight smile and glanced back at the little girl. "Her name is Illa."

"That's a beautiful name," Wren observed.

"So is Wren," she answered tentatively.

Wren smiled and cocked his head at her.

"Look, I am really sorry about crashing into you. I was trying to give her a bottle, and I must have looked away for a second and..." Liya sighed miserably and looked at him beseechingly. "I just moved to town, and I don't have much money right now, so I can't even pay for the damages. I just canceled my insurance. I just don't know what to do. Maybe I can pay you back in installments?"

"It's fine."

She narrowed her eyes at him and shook her head. "What?"

"It's fine. Don't worry about it."

"Did you hit your head against the dash or something?" she asked exasperatedly and motioned to the back of the BMW. "Look at it."

"I did," he said, his eyes never leaving hers.

Liya put her hands in her pocket. "Then how can you say that it's fine?"

"Because it is," he answered simply.

Liya's eyes filled up with tears again, and she lowered her gaze. Wren stepped closer to her.

"Please don't cry. It's fine. It's just a car," he said

Just a car, Wren? Did you really just say that?

"It's not *just* a car. It's a really nice BMW," Liya scoffed.

"You know cars?" he asked.

"The model name is right there," Liya answered and pointed to the logo.

"Right," Wren said as he suppressed a smile. "Would you and Illa like to go have coffee with me?"

"Oh, Illa doesn't drink coffee," Liya answered. "Oh, that's not what you meant. I'm sorry, I just..."

"Are you okay?"

She bit her lip and shook her head. "I just remembered, I have to be somewhere," she answered.

"Really? Or are you just blowing me off?" Wren asked, arching an eyebrow.

"I'm sorry," she cringed as she climbed back into her car and drove off, leaving Wren standing in the middle of the road. Luckily it was a small town, and the roads were not busy. He climbed back in his car and sped home to properly assess the damage to both his car, and his ego.

3

Liya smiled down at a sleeping Illa and rested her hand on the padded bumper that was arranged in a semi-circle around Illa to prevent her from rolling off the bed. The house didn't come furnished with a crib or anything of the sort, so Liya had to make do with what she had. She didn't mind having Illa sleep beside her in bed, as Illa's soothing abilities made her sleep soundly at night. Liya remembered the day that Illa was born like it was yesterday. Liya, being a petite young woman, was rather surprised that the birth was relatively easy. Even if it hadn't been, holding Illa in her arms for the first time made everything complete and perfect.

Liya reached out her hand to Illa and tenderly stroked her little hand which rested above her head. She quietly left the room and made herself a cup of coffee. As she sat down at the kitchen table, she recalled the events of the day. She still could not believe she had run into someone's car. She considered herself a really good driver, and before today she had never been involved in an accident. She shook her head. At least the guy she ran into wasn't a complete asshole about it.

Wren Wylde.

Wolf's Baby 31

The wolf.

Liya realized that he was a wolf even before she spoke to him. He looked out of place in a world that moved forward. He looked like he was in his early twenties, knowing well enough that he was hundreds of years old, at least. Another thing that gave him away was his car. No person that young, living in a small town like Bigfork, would own a car like that. Someone driving a car like that *wanted* to be noticed, acknowledged. Liya just didn't understand why.

All her life she was taught to hide from the humans, to blend in as much as possible and not to attract any attention, unwanted or otherwise, to herself or her pack members. Her parents had belonged to a smaller pack when she was younger, but the same rules applied.

Look after your family.

Never trust a human.

Never betray your own kind.

Those were the three things that were recited to her and to every wolf in the history of shifters, every single day of their lives.

Wren Wylde, however, seemed unfazed about drawing attention to himself, especially in that car, and with those eyes, a flawless set of perfectly straight teeth and a dimple in his left cheek that could melt the underwear right off any woman who looked at him.

Not that I looked at him that intensely, Liya shrugged to herself, not sure who she was trying to fool. He was all she could think about for the past few days, the memory of him burning a hole through her soul.

Wren Wylde. His name stuck in her mind like red wine on a white carpet, and it didn't help that she could vividly recall any memory she had ever had in her life. Some memories took precedence, of course, but now Wren Wylde forced his way inside her mind, and there was nothing she could do to stop it.

"What kind of name is Wren Wylde?" she muttered to herself.

Liya knew that a wren was a small brown bird who was rather inconspicuous, but was known for its loud and often complex songs. She remembered her father took her out into the fields behind her childhood home and let her listen to the wrens. Liya thought it was the most beautiful thing she had ever heard in her life and spent many afternoons in that very field. Some days she would lay out a blanket on the long grass, and she would lie there, watching the clouds float past her peripheral view of the sky, surrounded by the tall grass. She would listen to the sweet songs of the wrens, carried away to a better and less complex place.

Liya admired Mrs. Wylde, whoever and wherever she may be, for choosing the perfect name for her son. Wren had brown hair and brown eyes, just like the little bird, and even though he wasn't a tall guy, his song played pretty loud.

Now *his* song played in her mind, and she couldn't get rid of it.

Wren Wylde.

Somehow his name also sounded familiar to her, but she couldn't place it. Maybe she had overheard someone mentioning it. She still couldn't believe that he was so nice to her after she caused so much damage to his car. He even invited her to have coffee with him, which was also weird, but it didn't even come close to the strange feelings she felt inside her when she looked into his brown eyes.

She knew imprinting was different for every wolf, but the thought of imprinting with another wolf seemed a bit farfetched, especially since she wanted nothing to do with any male at this particular moment in time. She decided that it was

Wolf's Baby 33

probably just his comforting voice and the way he looked at her that made her feel like that.

Momentarily.

The last thing she wanted was to imprint on a wolf in another pack, especially since she was a Crescent. Although the Crescents were feared and respected—or feared more than they were respected—Liya knew all too well that Crescents were also one of the most hated packs in the country. Once Wren figured out that she was a Crescent, he'd most likely send her packing, or worse. Who knew what kind of hate his pack members carried in their hearts for the Crescents?

No, getting involved with Wren was *definitely* a bad idea. In fact, it was the worst idea she had ever had, and that included giving Hunter the benefit of the doubt that he would stop being a woman-beater and an all-around asshole.

Look how well that turned out, Liya, she scolded herself.

What she needed to do now was lay low, and no matter how much she wanted to run into Wren—not literally, like the last time—she knew she had to stay away.

Liya couldn't argue that he was incredibly hot, and charming at that, but she couldn't just blindly follow the laws of nature. She couldn't just move on so quickly, could she? Even though Hunter had been the man she had loved, or thought she had loved for a long time, her heart was too shattered to take on a new relationship. It wouldn't be fair to Wren, or Illa, or herself, for that matter. Maybe in time, but not now, and it didn't matter how strong the attraction between her and Wren was. Not even if she *did* imprint on him. Right now she needed to keep herself and Illa off the radar, and most importantly, safe.

Still, Liya had to try hard not to think about him, even though they had only met the one time. His eyes felt familiar, like she had seen him before, or maybe she was just struck by the power of the imprint. She didn't trust it at all. She never had.

She recalled the early days of her and Hunter's relationship and shivered as she remembered the clear signs that he was abusive, signs that she didn't see at the beginning. He had started out as jealous, which she had once thought was cute and endearing.

A FEW DAYS LATER, she was slowly walking up and down the aisles of the local store, pushing Illa in a shopping cart. Liya had made a whole list of things they needed for the house to ensure the cupboards were fully stocked.

Illa was playing with a musical toy in the shape of a microphone as Liya continued checking her list. She placed a few items in the cart and just as she was about to go around the corner, she bumped into someone.

"I'm so sorry," she murmured and glanced up into the unforgettable and undeniable pair of brown eyes of the one person she couldn't get out of her head.

"We have got to stop meeting like this," Wren said with a smirk in a low baritone which sent sensual shivers down her spine.

"You again," she forced a smile. She wasn't sure what she thought was going to happen, since Bigfork was a small town and it was quite inevitable for them to run into each other sooner or later.

"I could say the same about you," he said and raised a suspicious eyebrow. His expression immediately changed when he saw Illa and he smiled. "Hey, little girl. How are you?"

Liya glanced at the two of them having a conversation with one another that neither one of them understood. She *had* to admit, it was adorable seeing a big, tough-looking guy like Wren being cute with her one-year-old daughter.

Liya shifted her weight and cleared her throat. Wren looked at her and smirked.

"I'm sorry. Am I interrupting your shopping?" he asked.

"A little," she answered politely.

"Look, I just want to apologize for being a bit forward the other day," he said. "You don't even know me, and I invited you for a coffee."

"Right. I don't know you, and you don't know me," Liya said with a nod.

"I really want to change that, but if you're not up to it, I totally understand."

Liya narrowed her eyes and studied him for a second, or maybe five.

"Why?"

"Why what?" he asked.

"Why do you want to get to know me?" she asked.

"Well, I *could* use a really cheesy pick-up line telling you how you're the most beautiful woman I have ever seen, and you are, by the way," Wren said with a chuckle. "Or, I could tell you that being in a new place is scary and I know the feeling of being alone, which I wouldn't wish on anyone. In fact, I wish I had a friend when I moved here."

Friend? Does he want to be my friend?

"I almost believed you there," she said, rolling her eyes.

Wren laughed, a deep throaty laugh that matched him perfectly and Liya couldn't help but look at him in awe.

"You're funny," he said to her.

"So I've been told," Liya answered with a smile. "Look, I'd hate to turn you down twice, so I... we'd love to have coffee with you."

"That's the best news I've heard all day," he smiled.

"That's almost as cheesy as your first line," she said as she rolled her eyes and chuckled.

Later that afternoon, after Liya finished her shopping and unpacked the groceries at home, she and Illa went to the coffee bar that Wren had suggested. It was hidden away behind two corner shops, with a narrow hallway that led to the entrance, locked by a wrought iron gate. Only wolves were allowed inside, and it required a fingerprint scan to open. Liya thought it was really clever, and she was comforted by the fact that most of the population of Bigfork were wolves.

The inside of the cafe was earthy and rustic, and smelled of oak trees, freshly cut grass and coffee. Wren had arranged a table for them in the back, where there was a play area for kids. The cafe wasn't at all busy, as Liya assumed most wolves had jobs during the day.

Liya made sure that she wore a long shirt and used a bit of foundation to hide her tattoo, to avoid the risk of a complete overreaction from every single wolf in town. In the few days that she and Illa had lived in Bigfork, she had actually come to like the town.

"So, what's your deal?" he asked and studied her expression. "Why Bigfork?"

"We needed a change of scenery."

"Why? Was the old scenery getting a bit boring?"

"A bit," she answered, recalling the sight of Hunter's burning house in the rearview mirror.

"What about your family? Won't they miss you? Or Illa?"

"Why all the questions?"

Wren leaned closer to Liya and said, "Well, Bigfork is my town, and as the Alpha of my pack, I need to know the newcomers, and their reason for coming to this town."

"You're the Alpha," she stated blankly. "Wow, okay. I'm sorry I came into your town without discussing it with you first."

Wolf's Baby 37

"It's not a problem, Liya. I just like to know what's going on in my town," Wren said.

Liya looked away from Wren. "Sorry. I'm just a little jumpy."

"Why?"

When she turned back to him, she rubbed the back of her neck. "I'd rather not talk about it."

"Well, if you don't then I'd have to—"

"Kick me out of Montana," Liya interjected and glanced back at Illa in the play area to check if she was okay. Illa played happily in a shallow ball pit, throwing the balls at one of the caregivers.

"No," he said with a frown, "that wasn't what I was going to say. Why would I do that?"

"Because you're the Alpha. You have to look out for your pack," Liya answered.

"Only if there's a threat," he said and narrowed his eyes at her. "*Are* you a threat?"

"No, of course not."

Some might think so.

"Then I don't see a problem with it."

Liya's memories flashed in front of her eyes, and she inhaled nervously. Her eyes started to fill up with tears and she shook her head. "I ran away."

"From your pack? Were they hurting you?" he asked, concern instantly plastered across his face.

"No, the pack was fine."

"Then what?"

"I didn't run away from the pack. I ran away from my boyfriend," she finally said after a brief silence. "He was abusive, and I had to get out before..."

Wren's shoulders visibly slumped, and his eyebrows pushed together. "I'm so sorry."

Liya shrugged and looked at him. "Me too."

"You shouldn't be sorry. It's not your fault," Wren said.

"Well, I *did* set his house on fire, so it may be a little my fault if he's pissed off," she said, locking eyes with Wren.

Wren let out a low whistle. "You're a badass."

"Then why do I feel as afraid as I do right now? I'm always looking over my shoulder, hoping that he's not there."

"Has he made any contact with you?"

"No. I changed my number, got a new phone," Liya said. "I'm kind of an expert hider."

"You're a Concealer," Wren said simply and Liya nodded. "I've never met one before."

Liya smiled briefly. "It's not as glorious as people think. I feel like a coward, constantly hiding."

"We can't really choose our abilities, but it's what we do with them that counts, don't you think?" Wren said and raised his eyebrows at her.

"You're right," she answered with a nod and glanced down at her hand, at the layer of foundation that covered the tattoo. It was yet another sign that she was born a Concealer and would perish as one. It was all she knew. She hid away from the world, from the pain Hunter inflicted on her, and was hiding herself and Illa from Hunter. Now she hid her tattoo from Wren, who had been nothing but nice—too nice, actually—to her.

"So, isn't your girlfriend, or mate, or whatever, upset that you're having coffee with another woman?" Liya asked, changing the topic of conversation.

"Oh yeah, she's really upset," he chuckled and rolled his eyes. "So much so that she left town."

Liya glanced at him in mock astonishment and shook her head. "That's a bit of an overreaction."

"Just a little," he grinned.

"Okay, in all seriousness, though. Why are you still single?" she asked.

Wolf's Baby 39

Wren hesitated and looked in the direction of Illa in the play area. "She's really enjoying herself in that ball pit."

Liya averted her gaze to Illa, and she smiled. "Oh yeah. She does. She used to have one just like that..." Her voice trailed off, and she looked at Wren, who was watching her intently. "Do you always change the subject on purpose when you don't want to talk about something?"

"You're quite observant," he said with a smile. "I don't know. I've been alone for so long that it doesn't really bother me if someone is not around."

"Where's your family?" she asked.

His jaw clenched, and he answered reluctantly, "I don't know. I haven't seen them for a long time."

"Why not?" she asked, and when she saw the hesitation in his eyes, she cringed. "I'm sorry. That was probably too personal."

"No, it's fine. I haven't really talked about them in such a long time, or ever, actually," he admitted.

"Those are usually the difficult ones to tell," Liya pointed out.

"Mine is."

"We can talk about this another time," she said.

"Did you just agree to another date?" he asked and raised his eyebrows suggestively.

"This wasn't a date," she reminded him. "We were just two friends having coffee."

"Right," he said.

Liya glanced at her wristwatch and pouted. "I have to get Illa down for her nap, or I've got one terrible night to look forward to."

"Right. You don't want to mess up her routine," he said with a smile.

"Thank you," she said, and he raised an eyebrow at her in

puzzlement. "For being so nice," she clarified, "despite me ruining your car."

"It's not ruined."

"Right," she said, unconvinced.

While Wren took care of the check, Liya walked over to the ball pit. Illa held out her little arms to her mother, and Liya scooped her up and kissed her nose until Illa squirmed away.

They left the cafe and stepped out onto the curb. Wren walked Liya to her car, which still had a dented front bumper, and he openly cringed at the sight.

"I haven't gotten around to fixing it," Liya explained as she opened the back door and placed Illa inside her seat.

"I'll send you the number of my guy," Wren said. "He'll give you a really good price."

Liya clipped Illa into her seat and studied Wren with narrowed eyes. "It really *is* the same everywhere," Liya said vaguely.

"What do you mean?" Wren asked.

"The perks that come along with being an Alpha," Liya answered and closed the door.

"Oh yeah," Wren said and placed his hands on his hips. "Loads of perks."

Liya chuckled and looked at him. He was sexy as hell, especially in the waning daylight, and she had to fight the urge inside her to pin him against the car and kiss him.

Instead she composed herself and smiled at him. "Can I have your number?" she asked, surprised by her own boldness, and by the look on Wren's face, he was equally surprised.

"Sure," he said and took her phone that she handed to him. He punched in his number and gave it back to her.

"You didn't give me a fake number, did you?" she asked as she narrowed her eyes.

"The thought *did* cross my mind, but no," he answered.

Wolf's Baby

"Good night, Wren," she said as she climbed into her car.

"Good night," he answered with a smile.

Liya started her car and slowly drove away. As she looked in the rearview mirror at him, a smile ran across her lips.

Maybe she *would* stay in Bigfork after all. If anything, she had the Alpha on her side.

4

Wren had never given being alone much thought before today. Ever since the fire, he had been on his own, and never truly craved a companion to spend his time with. He was quite happy to be by himself, even though deep down inside he was miserable—but, of course, he would not disclose this to anyone. Today had been the first time that he wished he could spend more time with Liya and Illa, and it terrified him. The last time he had cared about someone, they were viciously ripped from his life. Not only his parents by the fire, but his brothers splitting up in different directions because they couldn't agree on anything. He had lost his entire family, and it hurt him. It hurt him so much that he wished he could take those memories from his mind and bury them as deep as he could. He didn't want to think about it anymore, he didn't want his nightmares to have such a hold over him, and most of all, he didn't want to carry the guilt and regret inside his heart any longer. For years after the fire he blamed himself for what had happened. If he had not made such a big deal about Cole not being suited to be the Alpha, would they have stuck together after the fire? If he had smelled the fire, or even those who set their home on fire, earlier, then their parents would have made it out alive.

Wren knew that there was no use in wishing to change the past, as it was done and buried. No amount of guilt or self-recrimination would change it. He knew this, but he silently tortured himself with a whip of guilt and a collar of remorse, dragging him down into his own personal hell.

Now there was light at the end of the tunnel in the form of a beautiful young woman and her adorable daughter.

Liya knew his pain even if she knew nothing about what had happened. She saw it in his eyes, because she had her own pain that she was dealing with. She had been terrified for a long time, and she had every right to be.

Even though Wren knew that they had imprinted when she ran into the back of his car, he also knew that it was not a good idea to take it further at the rate that he wanted to. She wasn't ready for something as serious as imprinting. She was barely ready to make new friends. He saw the distrust in her eyes, and he didn't blame her one bit. She was scared. Scared of being found by her ex-boyfriend, scared of being dragged back to her old pack, wherever that was.

Wren didn't even think to ask where she was from, and which pack she belonged to. Surely they noticed her disappearance. A sinking feeling appeared in Wren's stomach—he knew the protocol for a pack member who went AWOL, and he shivered.

No, I am not going to let that happen to her, he thought adamantly to himself.

Liya was his friend now, the only person he had ever opened up to, even if it was just a little bit. He had to protect her and Illa. She was a part of his pack now, and it was his duty to keep her safe.

As he stepped into his home, his phone rang, and he stared at the screen. He didn't recognize the number, but he answered anyway. Only a select few people had his phone number, and even when he didn't recognize the caller's number, it was always important.

"Wren Wylde," he answered.

"Wren, it's Liya."

Wren's heart stopped for a second, but he immediately sensed the panic and terror in Liya's voice. He also heard Illa crying in the background and instantly knew that something was wrong.

"Liya, what is it?"

"Someone broke into our house and..." Her voice was frantic, and she could barely form a cohesive sentence.

"Are you okay? Is Illa okay?" Wren asked, concern consuming every cell in his body.

"Yeah, we're okay. We just got home, and the whole house was turned upside down. Not literally, but everything is just everywhere," she stammered.

"I'll be right there," Wren said.

"Wren, wait. Don't you need my address?"

"No, I've got it covered."

"Wren?" Her voice was almost a whisper.

"Yes?"

"Be careful."

"Don't worry about me," he said and disconnected the call.

He rushed out the door, climbed in his car and drove to Liya's house, his nose leading the way.

It took him about five minutes to find her home, and he was surprised at how close she lived to his house. It was a cozy little

Wolf's Baby 45

unit that had a small porch at the back of the house overlooking the forested area, and he decided to quickly check it out for a scent before he went into the house. The area was dark and eerie, but Wren didn't pick up a scent at all, which was strange. It seemed like the most obvious way to get to her house undetected. He circled the area once more before heading to the house.

Inside, Liya was holding Illa, who still sobbed softly against Liya's shoulder. Liya swayed to and fro, whispering comforting words to Illa when Wren appeared in front of the glass door.

"It's open," Liya mouthed, and Wren slid the door open and stepped inside.

Liya wasn't kidding when she said that everything was everywhere. The couches and chairs were overturned, and all the contents of the drawers were scattered on the floor. The whole house was in complete disarray.

Wren approached Liya and placed his hand on her shoulder. "Are you okay?"

"We're not hurt, if that's what you want to know," she whispered.

Wren glanced at her reassuringly and lightly touched Illa's head. "Hey, little girl. You're okay."

To his surprise, Illa looked at him and held her arms out to him. Wren looked at Liya in surprise, and she nodded with a smile.

"She wants you," Liya whispered.

Wren smiled nervously and took Illa from her. Illa snuggled comfortably against Wren's chest as he wrapped his arms around her small body and he glanced at Liya again.

"Is this your first time holding a baby?" she asked with a suppressed laugh.

"Kind of, yeah," he whispered.

"Well, clearly you're a natural," Liya said with a smile.

Wren gazed at Liya, who looked at him in a way that made him feel too many emotions. He was holding onto the most important thing in her life, and she allowed it without question or hesitation.

Wren breathed in the soft scent of Illa and a warm feeling washed over his heart. He knew what it was, because he remembered the first time he felt it. He was a day old and the first time he looked at his mother that same feeling washed over him, and even though very few wolves could recall their memories from that far back, Wren remembered them.

Every one of them.

At times he wished he couldn't, but it was all so clear to him. The feelings, the smell of it all, but worst of all, the pain of knowing that he could never have that back. They were only memories now.

The warmth of Liya's hand on his shoulder pulled him out of the memory pool he wallowed in and he looked into her bright blue eyes, another pool he could drown himself in. Her eyes were a much safer place to drown in, and a small smile ran across his lips.

"She seems to really take to you," Liya whispered.

Wren said in a low tone, "You look surprised."

"I am. She doesn't like anybody, really. She's very picky."

"Good girl," Wren whispered to Illa and Liya smiled.

"Could I ask you a huge favor?" Liya asked, cringing slightly.

"What's that?" he whispered.

"Could Illa and I stay with you tonight? I don't feel very comfortable in this house and—"

"Of course," he said with a nod.

"Thank you," she whispered and placed her hand on his arm. "I'll go get a few things."

Wren nodded and watched as Liya left for the bedroom. He continued to sway side to side, although Illa was already fast asleep against his chest. Her little body was warm against his chest, and even though it was the first time he held a baby, it felt right. It felt like the most natural thing in the world and he couldn't help but smile. A few minutes passed and Liya came out of the bedroom with two overnight bags. She placed them on the floor and switched the lights off before turning to Wren, asking, "Are you ready?"

"Yeah, we can take my car, if that's okay."

"Sure, I'd just have to get Illa's car seat."

Within about five minutes, they arrived at Wren's house. The garage door opened and he parked the car inside.

Wren opened the door that led to the inside of the house, and they went in. He led Liya to the guest bedroom. Wren was thankful that he had a place for them to sleep, but even if he didn't, he would have more than willingly slept on the couch or on the floor to accommodate them.

In the dimly lit room, Wren watched Liya as she placed a U-shaped padded bumper on the bed and threw a fluffy blanket over it.

"You can lay her down," Liya said as she took out another blanket and a white stuffed rabbit toy from the overnight bag.

Wren nodded, although he could easily spend the entire night holding on to the precious little girl in his arms. He carefully laid her down, and Liya covered her torso with the blanket and placed the rabbit beside her.

"Will she be okay?" he asked as they closed the door almost all the way, and Liya nodded.

"Yeah, she'll sleep right through, thanks to you," Liya answered as they walked down the hallway and into the living room. "I think she just got a little upset because I was in a bit of a state."

"Are *you* okay?" Wren asked.

"I have no idea," she admitted. "I thought we were safe here and..."

"You *are* safe, here."

"But we can't stay here forever," Liya said with wide eyes.

"You stay as long as you need to, but we'll figure it out in the morning. We can go back and see if something was stolen or—"

"This wasn't a robbery, Wren. It was him. He came looking for us, or he sent one of his subordinates to track me down."

"You don't know that."

"You don't know Hunter," Liya said, and the fear she had for this guy was as clear as daylight.

"I know his type," Wren said and stepped closer to her. "I will not let him touch you or Illa. I promise you that."

Liya pursed her lips and a tear ran down her cheek.

Wren reached out his hand and brushed it away, the moisture immediately evaporating from his fingertip. "Why don't you go take a hot bath and I'll order some takeout."

"Sure, that sounds nice," Liya said. "Thank you for letting us stay here. I know it was completely unexpected and inconvenient because now you've got two strangers living in your house and—"

"It's not an inconvenience. I promise."

Liya smiled gratefully. "Okay, then."

"Bathroom is just on the opposite side of the hallway to your room," Wren said.

"Got it."

Wren watched as Liya turned away and walked down the hallway, entering the guest room. He smiled slightly and grabbed the phone from his pocket, dialing his favorite restaurant.

Wren placed his order and disconnected the call. He heard the water running in the bathroom, and he quietly walked to the guest bedroom, peeking around the door to check on Illa. She slept peacefully holding her stuffed rabbit, and Wren smiled.

He didn't care if he was turning into a real marshmallow, but fighting it would be futile as well.

After twenty minutes, the doorbell rang, and Wren answered it, collecting the food from Ben, the delivery guy, and handing over a few bills to him.

"Keep the change," Wren said.

"Thank you, sir," Ben said and rushed back to his car.

Wren's jaw clenched, recalling the way he and his brother had been taught to address their father when they were instructed to do something, or when they were in trouble and Luther scolded them. Wren still recalled his father's dark brown eyes, much like his own, and the stern expression that was permanently plastered to his face. Wren could count on his one hand the number of times that he saw his father smile, or laugh, for that matter. He often wondered how his mother, who was happy and free-spirited, ended up falling in love, marrying and having five children with such a pensive and stern man. Maybe it was because they each had something the other one lacked, or something like that. Maybe Mother Nature knew best and considered them to be a perfect match, hence their imprinting.

Wren closed the door and placed the bags on the kitchen counter. He walked down the hallway and stopped in front of the door.

"Liya?" he said quietly.

"Yeah?"

"The food's here."

"Okay, I'll just be a few more minutes," she answered from inside.

"Take your time," he said and quickly checked up on Illa again.

Wren was starving and he started to eat even before Liya came out of the bathroom. He was about halfway through his meal when she appeared from the hallway. She looked even more beautiful with her slightly damp hair and her flushed cheeks from the warmth of the hot water. Wren stared at her wordlessly, the intensity of his stare igniting a deep blush across her cheeks. She smiled slightly and looked down from the intensity of her emotions.

"I was just about to say that you didn't need to wait for me, but clearly you were starving," Liya said with a chuckle.

"I was. Sorry."

"You don't need to apologize. This is *your* house. We're guests here," she said and walked to the kitchen counter.

"I checked on Illa. She's off in dreamland riding a fuzzy white rabbit through the rainbows," Wren said

What? Seriously, Wren? he thought to himself, slightly embarrassed by the words coming from his mouth.

Liya smiled with bemusement and nodded. "This smells good," she said as she turned her attention to the food on the counter. "And judging by all the food on your face, it tastes good too."

"I have food on my face?" he asked with a mouthful of lo mein noodles.

Liya chuckled and grabbed a napkin. "Here, let me get that for you," she said and walked over to him.

As she reached her hand out to wipe the corner of his mouth, Wren's eye caught something on her wrist and his eyes instantly darkened.

"What is that?" he asked, but he didn't need her to explain. He knew exactly what it was.

"What is..." Her voice trailed off, and her eyes widened as she realized he'd seen it.

She tried to move her wrist away abruptly, but he grabbed it, and she cowered in his grasp.

"What is that?" he hissed with narrowed eyes. The cupid's bow of his upper lip pulled into a snarl, and his brown eyes narrowed as his body instantly and instinctively went on defense.

"Wren..."

"You're a *Crescent*?" he growled.

"Please, just let me explain," she begged in a small voice, not wanting to wake Illa.

Wren abruptly let go of her wrist and stood from the couch. "Then explain."

Liya straightened up and took a deep breath. "They're not my pack. They're Hunter's. He was born into the clan. I just joined because, well, we were together. I got the tattoo as a form of loyalty, to prove to Hunter that I wouldn't..."

"That you wouldn't what?" he asked impatiently. "Leave him?"

"Wren, I'm sorry."

"You know what the Crescents do to other packs, don't you?" he asked bitterly.

"I do, but I don't agree with it. They're power-hungry and evil and vicious, and not a second goes by that I am sorry for leaving. I *don't* want to be a part of that pack, Wren. I never really was a part of that pack to begin with."

"I don't trust you, Liya."

"I'm not going to kill you, and I'm not here to infiltrate your pack. I just wanted to get away from him, from all of them. I don't want Illa to grow up thinking that that kind of behavior is acceptable," Liya said, and a tear ran down her cheek. "I'm not like them; I swear to you."

Wren stared at her and he noticed the sincerity in her eyes. He *wanted* desperately to believe her, but this all seemed a little too coincidental.

The Crescents had tried more than a few times to take over the territories of other packs in the north, but had never succeeded, as it was too far from home. However, Wren and all the other Alphas knew that there would come a time when they'd all have to stand together against the Crescents. Until then, Wren was willing to fight to the death to make sure his territory did not fall into Crescent hands.

"How do I know you're telling the truth?" he asked after a brief pause.

"If I'm lying, you can take Illa," she answered, and her response shook Wren to the core. "You can do to her whatever you want."

"You'd never part with her," he pointed out.

"Exactly," she whispered.

Wren nodded.

It was at that moment that he knew she was telling the truth. No mother would ever willingly give up their child, especially not Liya.

"You could have told me sooner," he said to her, and his shoulders relaxed.

"When? In the supermarket? When I drove into your car?" she asked. "Hey, I'm Liya. I'm so sorry I drove into your car, but don't be too mad, because I'm a Crescent. I might just kick your ass," she joked sarcastically.

"That's ridiculous," he scoffed and looked at her. "You couldn't kick my ass even if you tried."

A small smile formed on Liya's lips and she nodded. "I'm not a fighter, remember?"

"So where was it before?" he asked and motioned to her hand. "The tattoo."

"I covered it with foundation," she said without making eye contact.

"A Concealer."

She sighed and said, "Exactly. I'm sorry I didn't tell you. I was just scared. I know how most other packs feel about the Crescents and I guess I just wanted to get away from all that. I didn't mean to upset you, or make you not trust me."

"It *did* take me by surprise. I was ready to attack."

"I saw that. Your eyes were so dark; it was actually terrifying. I wouldn't want to cross you, ever," she said, her voice still shaking a bit.

"So, Hunter is a Crescent," Wren stated, seeing Liya nod slightly. "Clearly he is pissed that you left and he wants you back."

"I'm not going back, Wren."

"Of course you're not. You belong here now, you and Illa belong here with..." His voice trailed off before he could finish the words that ran through his mind and his heart. He couldn't say it. He couldn't put such an enormous amount of pressure on her right now. She had enough to deal with; *they* had enough to deal with. "...with the rest of my pack."

Liya looked at him, a hint of disappointment in her eyes, but she didn't say anything. "Wren, can I just ask you something?"

"Sure."

"Why do you detest the Crescents?" she asked.

"They're savages. They take what they want without asking."

"No, why do *you* detest them?" Liya asked again, trying to be a little more specific than last time.

"It's a long story, and I don't feel like talking about it right now," Wren answered, looking away.

Liya nodded, and he stood up, walking down the hallway.

"Wren, where are you going?" she asked.

"To bed. It's been a long day. Good night," he said before disappearing into his own room and closing the door.

He heard Liya still moving around the house for a short while until she retreated to the guest bedroom. A silence filled the house, but inside Wren's mind, there was chaos so loud he was convinced that Liya could hear it.

5

No matter how hard Liya tried, she couldn't fall asleep. She was exhausted, but every time she closed her eyes, she was consumed by fear and guilt. Fear for her life and Illa's, and guilty that she had lied to Wren. Technically she didn't lie, but a lie of omission was still a lie. She rolled over onto her side and gazed at Illa, who would soon be waking up for her bottle and a diaper change. She slid off the bed, took Illa's bag and quietly made her way to the kitchen. She switched the kettle on and prepared a bottle for Illa. She poured the water into the bottle that was half filled with milk and dropped a teabag into it. She shook it briefly and waited for the teabag to soak for a bit.

Liya heard the floorboards creaking behind her and she whirled around with wide eyes and her heart pounding hard against her ribs.

"Holy crap, you scared me," she gasped.

"I could say the same about you."

Liya glanced at him and briefly bit her bottom lip. He looked ridiculously hot in a white t-shirt and a pair of black slacks. His hair was messy and disheveled, and his eyes were broody. He didn't look exhausted, just defeated. "I just had to make a bottle for Illa."

"Right. I'm not used to people in my house after midnight."

"I'm sorry if I woke you," she said.

"You didn't. I couldn't sleep," he muttered and ran his fingers through his hair. "Liya, look, about earlier—"

Before he could finish his sentence, Illa started to cry in the guestroom, and Liya quickly took the teabag out of the bottle, screwing the lid back on. "I'll be right back."

"Sure," he said simply, and Liya quickly rushed to the bedroom.

Illa had kicked the blanket off her and was not happy about it. Liya sat down beside her and gave her the bottle. Illa grabbed it with both hands and started to drink, while Liya quickly changed her diaper. When she was done, she placed the blanket over Illa's body and sat beside her until she fell asleep again.

As soon as Illa was asleep, Liya headed back to the kitchen where Wren sat on one of the chairs at the kitchen table.

"Is she okay?" he asked.

"Yes. She wanted her bottle. It's normal, she does it all the time, every morning at this time."

"Could we talk?" he asked and motioned to the empty chair beside him.

"Sure." Liya sat down and looked at him expectantly, waiting for him to start, since he had initiated this.

"I'm sorry I was a dick earlier. The Crescents are a sensitive subject for me," he said, the remorse evident in his dark eyes.

"It's okay. Really. It was a bit selfish of me to ask you something like that. Clearly it upsets you more than the average person, and I was insensitive to that," Liya said. "So I'm the one who has to apologize. I didn't mean to upset you, and if you don't want to talk about it, then it's okay. You don't have to until you're ready."

"Thank you, Liya."

"There is something that I'd like to talk about with *you*, if that's okay?"

"Sure."

"We imprinted, right? It wasn't just me? Please tell me it wasn't just me?" she asked.

Wren cracked a smile and shook his head. "It wasn't just you."

"Okay, good," she said and lowered her gaze. "I know what it is and what it entails and everything, but with everything going on, it's just..."

"Too much?" he asked.

"Yeah. Exactly. You're great, obviously," she stuttered, which he found oddly amusing, "and I am really lucky and grateful and relieved that I met you and we have this bond between us now, but the romance and the love stuff just has to wait. I don't know how *you* feel about it. Please stop me if I am not making any sense or if I'm being stupid or irrational."

Wren shook his head and placed his hand over hers. "You're not being irrational. I understand why you feel this way. You have Illa to think about, and her safety, and yours—"

"And yours, too."

"Mine?"

"Come on, Wren. You're a part of us now, and we're a part of you."

"That's a good way of putting it," he said.

"I'm sorry if this was not what you wanted to hear," Liya said.

"I understand. I've waited a really long time for you, and I can wait a little while longer," he answered.

His words took her completely by surprise— it was the most endearing and heartwarming thing anyone had ever said to her.

I definitely dated all the wrong men in the past, she realized with an inward cringe.

There was something in his eyes, something that she could not place, but it was undeniable. He sat across the table from her, and the attraction was stronger than she had ever imagined it would be, with anyone. Not even the first time she and Hunter had sex had she felt such intensity, and it *was* pretty hot.

There was also something about the way he looked at her in the dimly lit kitchen. The gentle rays of the moon shone through the window, accentuating the lines of his face and creating swirls of sensuality inside her veins. She didn't even realize her breathing was ragged until he stood slowly, and she mirrored his action.

As the desire built up inside her, her hands started to shake, and she took a deep breath.

Fuck it.

Driven by her impulses, all the desire that she had tried to contain inside her for the last week since crashing into his car burst open at the seams, and she didn't care whether she was about to do something that she had promised herself she wouldn't do. She wrapped her arms around his shoulders, pulling him roughly towards her, and kissed him.

His strong arms wrapped around her waist, and he kissed her in return. In one smooth move, he scooped her up in his arms, but instead of heading to the bedroom, or even the living room, he placed her on the kitchen table. His hands traveled all over her body, and her senses were ready to explode.

Not just her senses.

She moaned against his mouth as his hands cupped her breasts and she leaned her head back, relishing the sensations of being touched by him. He ripped open the front of her shirt, and she heard a few buttons fall onto the wooden floor below her, but she didn't care.

Liya slipped her hands under Wren's shirt and felt his rock-hard muscles ripple at her touch. Her hands traveled down, and

Wolf's Baby   59

the hardness continued down to his crotch. She fondled the front of his slacks, and he let out a deep and sexy groan.

Wren slipped his fingers under the waistband of her pants, as well as her panties, and pulled them down in one smooth motion. She did the same with his slacks and looked into his eyes which were practically on fire.

So was she, in all the right places.

He kissed her again, lowering her down onto the table, and grabbed her hips. She wrapped her legs around him as he thrusted into her with a motion that was tender and urgent at the same time.

She gasped at the feeling of being filled up by him and arched her back. His thrusts were slow and deep, but he soon increased them to an intense rhythm which threw her over the edge multiple times. His skin on hers was magical, carnal and satisfying in a way that was beyond anything she'd ever experienced.

Liya groaned at his increased pace and felt him move deeper and deeper inside her. She dug her nails into the skin on his back, and he grabbed the edge of the table with a groan. His body was now pressed up against hers and she moaned in his ear. His last three thrusts were slow and hard and he slowly turned his face towards her, allowing their noses to touch. They stared at one another while catching their breaths, not moving at all. Wren pushed himself up midway and ran his fingers down her shoulders, down her chest and to her stomach.

"You're beautiful," he whispered, his voice hoarse.

Liya simply lay there, looking at him with the happiest smile on her face, but once again she didn't care. She was fully satiated for the moment, and was enjoying the view of the most amazing man in the world.

He bit his lip and pulled away from her. Liya noticed the

slight detachment in his eyes and she reached out to him. He briefly touched her hand but still stepped away.

Liya sat up and frowned at him. "Wren?"

He looked at her as he pulled on his slacks. "You should go check on Illa," he said before he disappeared down the hallway.

Liya slid off the table and quickly got dressed. She crossed her arms and sighed to herself. She felt like a hypocrite. *She* had been the one who said that she wanted to wait with all the romance and love stuff, yet *she* was the one who initiated the sex.

The mind-blowing, soul-devouring sex.

On the kitchen table.

Nice going, genius, she thought to herself as she walked down the hallway. Wren's door was closed, and she heard the water running in the shower. She stood in front of his door for a few seconds, not sure whether she should wait for him to come out, or if she should call it a night and go to bed. She wasn't at all tired after being sexed up by him, but she knew she needed to sleep or she'd be exhausted later. She walked back to her bedroom and closed the door. She smiled at her sleeping baby on the bed and lay down beside her.

She fell asleep much quicker than she thought she would and woke up to a bright and sunny bedroom, with Illa lying next to her, playing with her feet.

"Good morning, baby girl," Liya said with a smile.

After changing Illa's diaper again, Liya made her another bottle. She scooped Illa up in her arms and stepped out of the room.

The entire house was bright, which Liya didn't expect at all. Her house had never been as bright and as she glanced at the ceiling, it all made sense. There was a large skylight in the living area, which contributed greatly to the amount of light filling the house.

"Look how pretty, Illa," Liya said as she pointed to the sky

Wolf's Baby 61

and the clouds through the glass. "Look at the pretty clouds, baby."

"Morning," she heard Wren say and she spotted him in the kitchen.

"Hey."

"How did you two sleep?" he asked, as if nothing had happened.

"Good," Liya answered, playing along. "Illa slept like a log after that bottle."

"You?" he asked and looked at her intently. "Did you manage to get any sleep after..."

"Yeah. That bed was really comfortable."

"Good," he answered and shifted his weight uncomfortably.

"Wren?" she asked as he took Illa from her and he looked at her wordlessly. "Why is this so weird?"

"I don't know," he shrugged. "Maybe it was because you said to wait, and we didn't."

"*I* didn't. I was the one who initiated—"

"We didn't," he said firmly. "I wouldn't have allowed you to stop, and neither would you have allowed me to stop."

He was right. There was no possible way she would have been able to stop, even if she wanted to. "I'm sorry. It was a mistake."

"Untimely and irresponsible, but not a mistake."

"You're just trying to convince me to do it again," Liya said, biting down her lower lip trying to suppress a smile.

"Maybe," he said and tilted his head to the side, a small smile playing on his lips.

"You're really cocky."

"Maybe," he smirked. "I was thinking we could go somewhere today. You, me and Illa."

"Where?" she asked.

"I know of this great little town just north of here. They have this bakery there, and everything tastes amazing."

"Maybe another time. You said we could go by my house and assess the damage," Liya said.

His smile faded slightly and he nodded. "Right."

"We can go some other time; I promise. I just need to see if it really was Hunter or one of his subordinates who ransacked my house," Liya said.

"Okay, but I will hold you to your word," he said with a nod. "But first, breakfast."

"That sounds good. I am starving," Liya said as she sat down at the table—*the* table—and smiled slightly. As she shifted her chair closer, she heard a sound and glanced at the ground. One of her buttons lay on the floor right by the foot of her chair and she reached down to retrieve it. She studied it for a short while and shoved it into her pocket as Wren placed a plate of food in front of her.

"Wow, look at that," she said with wide, impressed eyes. "I didn't know you could cook."

"My mother taught me," he said.

"Ah, that's nice."

Wren smiled briefly and said, "I forgot to ask, what does Illa eat?"

"She eats anything, but she especially likes avocados, bananas, and mashed potatoes," she answered and noticed the disgusted look on his face. "Not together."

"Oh, okay. That's a relief," he said and glanced at Illa, who seemed very amused and mesmerized by his disheveled hair, tugging at it every chance she got.

Liya watched him with her daughter and still couldn't believe that Illa was so comfortable with him. Furthermore, she couldn't believe that he was so comfortable with Illa. He had made it very clear on numerous occasions that he had never held a baby before, and now he treated her like his own.

In a way, Illa *was* his daughter now, and Liya knew that he would be a much better father to her than Hunter would ever be. Wren and Hunter were just two completely different people, which made it impossible to compare them, but ultimately Hunter was a bad guy, and Wren was not.

"It's rude to stare, you know," Wren suddenly pointed out.

"Says who?" she asked.

"My mom used to say that to me a lot."

"Can I just point out something without being scolded?" she asked as Wren brought his own plate to the table and sat down with Illa on his lap.

Illa grabbed a slice of toast and started to chomp away on it.

"Sure," he said eventually and looked at Liya.

"For someone who doesn't want to talk about your family, you talk about your mother a lot," Liya said.

"That's true, but she was wonderful, and it'd be an injustice to her if I *didn't* think about her," he answered.

"No one said you shouldn't think about her, Wren," Liya said and looked at him apologetically. "When did she die?"

"In the fifties."

"The 1950s?"

"Yes."

"I'm so sorry," Liya said and placed her hand over his, which was resting on the table. "What happened?"

"*That*," he said, sliding his hand out from under hers, "is not something I am ready to share with you."

"I understand. The last thing I want is for you to tell me something that you're not ready to," she said. "There are things that I'm also not quite ready to talk about yet. Most of it involves Hunter and the Crescents, which was when my life turned into the raging shit-storm it was up until now."

"Are you kidding? It still is," he chuckled, and she joined in his laughter. Even Illa started to giggle. "She is so adorable, and she looks just like you, except for the hair, though. I think she got that from me," he said with a wink.

"She had to get *something* from you, right?" Liya said with a smile.

"Exactly," he said. "Alright, ladies, eat up. We have a lot to do today."

"What do you mean?" she asked. "We're just going to the house—"

"Yeah, but you need a few things if you're going to stay here with Illa," he said.

"Here? No, we can't just move in here with you," she said, crinkling her nose.

"Why not? There's plenty of room. Plus, I know you two are safe here. I have a security system, cameras everywhere—"

"Everywhere?"

"Yes," Wren said with a smirk.

"Do they record *all* the time?" Liya asked.

"Yes," he answered again.

Liya smirked and shook her head. "You better delete that."

"Don't worry. I did, but it *is* permanently etched in my mind, and some other places," he said as he looked her up and down.

"You shouldn't be talking about *that* with my daughter in the room," Liya said under her breath.

"She's too busy stuffing her little face with my breakfast," Wren said dryly as Illa grabbed the piece of breakfast potatoes from Wren's plate.

6

When Wren noticed the mess last night, it didn't seem too bad, but standing in Liya's house the next morning, in broad daylight, it was even worse. Everything was thrown on the floor; the couches were overturned, pillows were on the floor. Books and papers were strewn around the room. Even the kitchen cabinets and the fridge were emptied. It was going to take the whole day to clean this up, and Wren definitely didn't want Liya to spend the entire day there. He had to do something, so he took his phone out of his pocket and dialed a number.

As it rang in his ear, Liya entered from the bathroom, holding Illa with a helpless expression on her face. When she saw he was on the phone, she gave him a questioning look, but he motioned to her to give him a minute.

"Hey, Wren."

"Luca, hey. I need a favor."

"Anything."

"How soon can you get your cleaning crew ready?" Wren asked and looked at Liya.

"How soon do you need it?"

"Right away, if possible," Wren answered.

"I'll assemble and send them right over."

"I'm not at home. Send them to Eagle Bend Drive. My car is out front," Wren said and lowered his gaze. "Make sure they're not being watched or followed."

"We always do. Anything else?"

"If you could get Shea to come along, that would be great," Wren said as he turned away.

"Are you sure about that?" Luca asked with concern.

"Yes. I am sure," Wren said tightly.

"You know what happened the last time you were in the same room as she was."

"I remember, but we're both adults."

"You were adults that time as well."

Wren sighed and ran his free hand through his hair. "Could you please just do as I ask?" he growled.

Out of the corner of his eye he noticed Liya freeze and stared at him with wide eyes. He hadn't realized just how loud his growl was and he sighed again.

"Will do. I'm sorry for questioning you."

"It's fine, just get them here," Wren grumbled and disconnected the call. He glanced up and looked at Liya, who still held Illa in her arms.

"Is everything okay?" she asked.

"Yeah. Sorry about that growl."

"It's okay. Nothing I haven't heard before," she shrugged. "You're sending a cleaning crew here?"

"Yes. This place is going to take the whole day to clean and get back to the way it was," he explained.

"It's fine. I can just do it myself."

"No, I insist," he said and looked at her. "They're already on their way."

Wolf's Baby 67

"What kind of cleaning crew shows up at your door five minutes after you call them?" she asked.

"The kind who knows that defying the Alpha's orders can have dire consequences," he said ominously.

"Wow, you're really enjoying being bossy, aren't you?" she asked.

"I'm not being bossy," he answered defensively.

"Then why the growl?"

"You ask a lot of questions," he said and turned away.

"I'm allowed to, aren't I?"

"Sure, but it doesn't mean that I will answer all of them."

"Has anyone ever told you how unbelievably stubborn you are?" she asked.

"Yeah, everyone," he answered with a smirk. "Why?"

Liya shook her head and glanced at Illa, who seemed amused by the whole conversation. "Do you *believe* this guy, baby girl?"

Illa giggled and shook her head, which made both Liya and Wren chuckle.

"Look, I don't want you to be in this house anymore. That's why I asked Luca to assemble the cleaning crew," he explained. "Luca is my Delta, and he's in charge of keeping everything 'clean'."

"And by 'clean', you mean more than just clean houses," she said, arching an eyebrow.

Wren nodded and approached her slowly. "Luca knows his job and so does his team. They'll have this place looking *exactly* the way it was. There will be no trace that you and Illa were ever here, and they even make your scent disappear from the area."

"Really? They can do that?"

"Yeah. Well, Shea can."

"Who's Shea?" Liya asked.

"She's..." Wren swallowed audibly and looked at Liya.

"What, is she your wife or something?" Liya joked.

"No, we used to go out, but it was a long time ago."

"A wolf ex-girlfriend. Wow."

Wren let out a deep breath. "Liya..."

"It's fine. It's not like we're... I mean, you and I, we're just..."

Wren raised his eyebrows and looked at her expectantly.

"It's fine," she fobbed him off and turned away.

"Fine," he said with a nod.

Clearly she wasn't as fine as she said she was, but he wasn't going to make her admit it. He just hoped that Shea was in a better mood than the last time he saw her.

A knock on the front door made them both jump and before he could do anything, she handed Illa over to him and walked to the front door.

"Liya..."

"What?" she asked as she looked at him over her shoulder.

"Nothing," he said and glanced at Illa, who started to tug at his hair again.

He heard Luca's voice and within a few seconds, the crew of five people, including Shea, stepped inside the living room where he stood.

"Wren," Shea said to him.

"Shea," he said simply and noticed Liya looking at Shea in slight disapproval.

Women...

"What's with the baby?" Shea asked.

"She's *mine*," Liya said defensively as she stepped forward and took Illa from Wren, "and her name is Illa."

Shea put her hands up and glanced at Wren.

Oh shit...

"Okay, so we're heading out," Wren said briskly and glanced at Luca. "You've got everything covered, right?"

"Of course," Luca nodded.

Wolf's Baby   69

"Good. Call me when you're done," Wren said and looked over at Liya. "Are you ready to go?"

"Sure," Liya responded and she followed him as he left through the front door.

The drive back to his house was a bit awkward and uncomfortable, and as they stepped inside, he turned to her.

"Liya-"

"Shea is really pretty," she said.

"I suppose," he muttered.

Talking about Shea was the *last* thing he wanted to do, especially with Liya.

"How long were you together?" she asked as she quickly changed Illa's diaper on the couch.

"A while, although some days it felt like a damn eternity," he sighed.

Liya paused to look over at him with a look of confusion on her face.

"*That* was a joke."

"Not a very good one," she muttered.

"Okay, I'm not going to pretend that something is not up with you, so I expect you not to either," he said as he turned to face her.

She zipped up Illa's onesie and looked at him. "I don't know what you're talking about."

Wren watched as Illa slid off the couch and crawled across the floor. His gaze returned to Liya and he placed his hands on his hips. "I think you know."

Liya eyes darted from Wren to Illa as she played with her hair.

"I don't know why you're even acting the way you do. We've been over for a long time now, and I would rather saw off both my legs than even think of getting back together with her. We're just not good together. She drove me crazy, and not in the way you do," Wren said.

"I drive you crazy?" she asked.

"In a good way."

Liya smiled briefly and nodded. "I'm sorry, I guess I was just a bit threatened by her, even though..."

"You don't have to be," Wren assured her.

"I don't have to be friends with her, do I?" Liya cringed.

"Oh, hell no. She's not the type of person I would want you hanging around with. I mean, she's a loyal member of the pack and she does an amazing job at removing scents and all that, but she's just..." Wren thought for a moment and looked at Illa on the floor by his feet.

"She's just what?"

Wren looked up and at Liya. "She's just not you."

Liya's head arms dropped down to her sides. "You can't say stuff like that."

"I know, but I can't help it," he said and walked up to her. He took her hands and slipped his fingers in the spaces between hers.

"Wren, we can't do this," she murmured.

"I don't understand how you can keep yourself as composed as you do," he whispered in her ear.

"I'm glad you think I'm composed. I'm ready to burst," she answered.

"I know the feeling," he said, and she chuckled. "Can't we just..."

"What?"

"Can I just kiss you right now?" he asked, ready to go down on his knees and beg.

Liya rubbed her lips together before parting them and nodded. "Go ahead."

Relief washed over Wren as he pulled her close to him and

kissed her. He could practically hear the fireworks in the background as he tasted her against his tongue. The heat of her touch set his skin on fire, and he had to force himself to simmer down. After all, Illa was still in the room.

Wren pulled away slowly and stepped back, his breathing just as ragged as hers. "I think that's enough for now."

"I think so, too," she panted.

"We, um, should get going. I want to get a few things for the house," he said, his eyes still on her.

"Sure," she said with a nod as she took a few steps back. "I'll be right back."

As Wren lowered his gaze, he noticed the shift in his jeans and he awkwardly adjusted himself into a more comfortable position. Unfortunately for him, Liya walked into the room at that moment and a smirk appeared on her lips.

"I'm glad to see that I wasn't the only one who needed a minute," she said as she looked up at him through her lashes.

IT WAS AFTER MIDNIGHT, and Wren sat in the dark living area, staring out in front of him. The day had been rather fun, but he silently vowed that he would *never* go shopping with Liya ever again. She was indecisive and took *forever* to decide that she didn't want *any* of the things she tried on. At the end of the day, they came home with more things for Illa than for her, which she assured him was quite normal.

A smile formed on his lips as he continued to stare into the darkness. Since he had met Liya and Illa, his life had changed tremendously, and he could not imagine not having them in his life. Illa was such a little bundle of joy and energy and he already loved her with his entire being. He considered her to be his daughter, and no one could convince him otherwise. Liya was an amazing woman, and although he didn't really know much about her past or her family, he couldn't imagine himself with someone else, and was sure that whatever she told him about her or her family wouldn't have any impact on how he felt about her.

It wouldn't matter anyway. Mother Nature wouldn't have allowed him to imprint on someone with whom he was incompatible, or someone whom he himself would not approve of. Imprinting was much stronger than love. It was forever, longer lasting and stronger than any kind of true love could ever be.

The floorboards creaked behind him and he glanced over his shoulder. Liya, who was on her way to the kitchen, saw him sitting in the dark and turned to him.

"Hey," she whispered as she approached him. "Is everything okay?"

"Yeah. I just couldn't sleep. It's a normal thing for me. I've never been a good sleeper," he said.

"I forgot how to be a good sleeper even before Illa was born. It's hard to get comfortable when you're pregnant," she said. "Can I sit with you?"

"Sure," he said and patted the empty spot beside him.

She smiled slightly and sat down on the soft couch. "Is there something on your mind?"

He eyed her and pouted slightly. "There's always something on my mind."

"If that's another cheesy line, I'm going back to bed," she threatened.

"No lines. Apparently, I'm better than that," he said and propped his head up with his hand, his elbow resting on the armrest of the couch.

"Yes, you are," she chuckled. "Besides, you already got the girl."

"That is true," he said and there was a brief moment of

Wolf's Baby

silence. "You asked me why I hated the Crescents and I didn't want to answer you. Do you want to know why?"

"Sure," she answered simply.

"Because my hatred for them runs deeper than anyone can ever imagine," he answered. "My family and I lived on a beautiful piece of land in Minnesota, and it was the most beautiful house I had ever known. Each of us had our own bedroom, and it was great," he said with a nostalgic smile.

"How many siblings do you have?" she asked, curious to hear about his family, and relieved that he was finally opening up to her about his life before Bigfork.

"I have four brothers," he answered and Liya's eyes widened. "I'm the middle one."

"Wow, that's a lot of kids, and all boys too."

"Yeah. Each of us got one of the five senses. Cole, the eldest, got taste, Kodiak got touch, which in my opinion, is the best one of them all."

"Why is that?"

"He can feel emotions of anyone he chooses to, and he can intensify it, or numb it completely. He can even manipulate feelings and emotions," Wren answered.

"Why would you want to do that?"

"It's an amazing ability," Wren contended.

"Maybe the part where he can take away someone's pain, or increase someone's happiness, but feeling what others are feeling can just be overwhelming."

"I never thought of it that way," Wren mumbled. "Anyway, I got smell; Scout got sight and River got hearing."

"The five senses. That's pretty awesome," she smiled.

"Yeah."

"Where are they now?" she asked. "I know you said you didn't know, but—"

"I don't know where they are. I've heard their howls in the

distance on the nights where the wind blew in from the east and the north, and once I even thought I heard them coming from the south, but I'm not as good at hearing as River is."

"What happened that kept you from staying in contact?"

"One night in the fifties, our house was set alight and it burnt to the ground, with our parents still inside. They never made it out," Wren said and he paused, feeling the emotions bubble up inside him. His eyes filled with tears as he heard the screams that were permanently etched inside his mind and would probably stay there until the day he took his last breath.

Liya's eyes widened and she stared at him silently before bringing her hand up to her face. "I am so sorry. I... I don't even know what to say."

"You don't have to say anything," Wren said and stared at his hands which rested on his lap.

"Do you know who would do such a horrible thing to your family?" she asked.

Wren nodded slowly and looked at her. "The Crescents."

Liya nodded as well and said, "That doesn't surprise me. They're heartless enough to do something like that."

"It didn't surprise me either, but then it occurred to me that the Crescents do things for a reason," Wren said, and Liya looked at him, startled.

"You think that they tried to kill your entire family for a *reason*?" Liya asked, and he nodded. "For what reason?"

"I was hoping you could tell me."

Liya frowned at him. "I might have been a member for little over four years, Wren, but I hardly know things like that."

"You must have heard something," Wren said hopefully.

"No, I didn't. I tried to distance myself as much as possible from those people. They're a bunch of savages that don't give a damn about anyone but themselves," Liya said. "The only way

Wolf's Baby

they would go through all that trouble is if someone in your family majorly pissed them off."

Wren looked at her and his eyes widened slightly.

"Do you know if anyone was involved in something shady with them?" Liya asked.

"No, not at all."

"Did any of your brothers—"

"No, they would never do that. They detested them as much as I still do. It was because of them that we had to move away from Minnesota the first time around. I always suspected my brother Cole knew something I didn't, but I never got him to admit to anything. It doesn't matter. We separated, and my family is here now, with my pack."

"Tell me more about the night you split up."

"It's a long story," Wren sighed.

"I've got time," Liya said and looked expectantly at Wren.

Wren proceeded to tell her the story from the night his parents died, and the last time he saw his brothers.

7

Liya glanced at Wren, who sat motionless on the couch beside her. The story he had told her about his family made the hairs on the back of her neck stand on edge. Wren's eyes were drawn and Liya was almost too afraid to ask or say anything.

"I always suspected the Cole and my father were trying to recruit Crescents to our pack, but I never knew for sure. Actually, I am not even sure who burned our house down. It's all a mystery to me," Wren eventually said.

"And neither of them would tell you, even if you asked?" she questioned, her voice feeling small.

"No," he answered simply.

"Not even now?" she asked.

Wren looked at her with glistening eyes. He was quiet for a few seconds before saying, "No."

"How do you know?"

"Because I know what Cole is like. He pledged loyalty to my father first out of all of us, and he's not going to go back on that. That's one of his traits—when he promises something, he'll keep his word for as long as he's alive."

"It would make sense why you guys had to leave. Maybe the Betas, or even the Alpha found out what your father was doing and he just wanted to protect his family."

"Why are you defending my father?" he asked. "Do you know anything about this?"

"No, I just want you to consider that maybe your dad and Cole weren't as bad as you thought, or think," Liya answered and reached out to take his hand. "You don't want the memory of your father to be one that makes you upset or ashamed. I'm sure your father loved you, all of you."

"No, he died with that secret."

"Wren, that's not fair."

"You didn't know him, Liya. He was..." Wren grumbled and ran his free hand through his hair.

"He was your father, Wren, and it doesn't matter if he was a bad guy, or how much you think he hated you, because he didn't. I know that if he was alive today and he could see you, the Alpha of your own pack and how great you were doing, he'd be really proud of you, and so would your mother," Liya said, her voice softly caressing his insides.

"My mom was always proud of me, even if I didn't do anything," he whispered.

"I can see how she would be," Liya whispered in return.

Wren glanced at her, and she knew that his heart thawed slightly as her words struck a chord inside him. His eyes were luminous in the darkness and all she wanted to do was hold him. She shifted closer to him and held her hands out to him. "Come here," she murmured and he looked at her reluctantly.

"Fine, then," she said as she sat on his lap and put her arms around him.

"What are you doing?" he asked.

"I'm hugging you because clearly you need it," she answered.

"What makes you think I need a hug?" he asked.

"The way you look at me with those doe-brown eyes of yours. They're filled with pain and regret, guilt and feelings that you were never good enough," she answered, holding him tightly against her.

His arms folded around her waist and he held onto her.

"You are good enough, and don't you ever forget that, okay?" she whispered.

She felt him nod against her, and he held onto her even tighter. After a few seconds, Liya heard his soft sobs, and her heart broke from all the pain and self-recrimination washing over him.

"It's okay," she whispered to him, over and over, consoling him.

She wasn't sure how long they sat like that, but when his grip on her loosened, she pulled away, still sitting on his lap, and looked down at him. His eyes were red but he was still beautiful in all his vulnerability.

Without a word, Wren gripped her waist and lifted her off him onto the couch and stood up.

"Wren..."

He held his hand up in the air as he walked out of the room and disappeared down the hallway. Liya stood up after a second but didn't follow him. She knew that he needed a bit of space, so she went to check on Illa, who was sleeping soundly in the room, her arms stretched out to the sides, resembling a starfish. Liya smiled as she carefully felt her diaper, but it was surprisingly okay. She noticed the full and untouched bottle beside Illa and watched her sleeping baby for a while.

She heard Wren walk past the bedroom and back into the living area and she kissed Illa on the cheek. "I love you so much," she whispered before leaving the room.

Wren stood in the middle of the room with his hands on his

hips. His hair was damp around his hairline and his eyes weren't as red as they had been. Liya approached him and asked, "Are you okay?"

His eyes were dark and broody as he looked at her, not saying a word. She took another step towards him and smelled his scent. His closeness was overwhelming, more than before, and she knew it was because of all his emotions that had now been brought to the surface. Judging by the look on his face, he was overwhelmed by it as well.

"Wren," she asked again, "are you okay?"

"I'm sorry."

"For what? You don't have to apologize to me, especially not because you showed your emotions," Liya said to him in a reassuring tone.

"The last time I cried like that was the night of the fire," he admitted. "That night I promised myself that I wasn't going to get swept away by my emotions again, because I knew that it didn't help me one bit. Crying and getting emotional wasn't going to change or rectify the situation."

"You're not a machine, Wren. You have feelings too, and it's okay to let those feelings out once in a while," Liya said and touched his hand.

"So now I should be good for another few decades," he mumbled.

"Hey," she said and pulled him closer to her, "you don't have to hide when you're around me. I'm the Concealer, remember?"

"Thank you for putting up with me," he said gratefully.

"If I don't, then who will?" she joked. "But seriously, Wren, I'm here, and neither your moods nor your emotional overloads are going to scare me away. You're stuck with me."

Wren put his arms around her and smiled weakly. "I can live with that," he said and touched her chin, tilting it up. He leaned in closer to her and kissed her on the lips, tenderly and filled with emotion.

They spent the rest of the night talking on the couch until finally, they fell asleep in each other's arms. The warmth of Wren's nearness heated her entire body, and she felt completely and utterly safe with him.

~

LIYA WASN'T sure what time it was, but she was shaken awake by a loud crashing sound. Her body jolted upright at the same time Wren's did.

"What was that?" she asked.

Illa's cries made her head snap up and they rushed down the hallway. They barged into Illa's room and found the window shattered, shards of glass on the ground beside the bed. Illa sat upright, crying and holding her arms out for Liya. Liya rushed to her and scooped her up, consoling her.

"Careful of the glass," Wren cautioned as he stepped closer to the window.

"They know we're here," Liya said as she held Illa and turned to Wren, who already had his phone against his ear.

"Sutton, we have a problem."

Liya didn't hear the rest of the conversation, as she was too focused on the brick that lay at her feet. Her eyes filled with tears and she backed away.

"Sutton and a few of the pack members are on their way," Wren said and turned to her. "Liya, what is it?"

"Look at that." Liya pointed to the brick by her feet and Wren crouched down to retrieve it.

"I know that smell," he said with wide eyes.

"Hunter's scent? You *know* Hunter's scent?" Liya asked with a horrified expression on her face. "How?"

Wolf's Baby 81

"I have no idea," he answered and stood upright. "I've smelled it before; I just don't know where."

"Well, that's not comforting," she muttered.

"Wait, here's something written on the back," Wren said and showed the back of the brick to Liya.

"I want her," Liya read with a gasp and held Illa a little tighter against her chest. "No. He's not getting her. He'll have to pry her from my cold, dead hands. There is absolutely no way that I am giving Illa to him."

"I know. I won't let you either," Wren said and touched Illa's head. "Are you okay, little girl?"

Illa looked at him and held her arms out to him. Wren scooped her up in his arms and held her tight. "It's okay. I won't let anything happen to you, okay?"

Illa placed her head on his shoulder and Liya blinked her eyes several times, suppressing the tears that already threatened to run down her cheeks. Wren glanced at her, and his eyes glowed in the moonlight.

"I mean it, Liya. I won't let anything happen to either one of you. You're my family now, and I'm not going to let the Crescents take you away from me," he said. "Not again."

Liya nodded and leaned against him as she stared at the broken window.

"They're here," Wren said suddenly and Liya's eyes widened in terror.

"Who? Hunter?"

"No, I asked Sutton and a few of the Zetas to come over, for protection," Wren said.

"Okay," was all Liya could say. Words failed her as the fear of losing Illa almost consumed her, but she knew that neither she nor Wren would allow that to ever happen. She followed Wren, who still held Illa, as he walked to the front door and opened it. In the doorway stood Sutton, a tall, dark-haired guy with bright blue eyes, and four others whose names she didn't know.

"Come on in. Thanks for coming so fast," Wren said as he stepped aside, allowing them to enter.

Liya noticed the strange expressions on the others' faces as they looked at Wren holding Illa, and Liya felt rather honored that Wren had cozied up to Illa in such a way, since he wasn't the emotional type.

"You all know Liya," Wren said and motioned to Liya.

Liya smiled politely and looked at them.

"This is Jace, Krew, Ash and Torin," Wren said, motioning to each of them.

"Hey," Liya said with an awkward smile and looked at the four of them standing in front of her. They were all brawny guys with broad shoulders and had the type of pensive looks on the faces that would make any person think twice about approaching them. They were tough, Liya could see it, and they wouldn't take any shit from anyone, which was a good thing.

"This is Illa, Liya's daughter," Wren said with a smile, and Illa smiled at them as well.

"She's cute," Sutton said.

"Thank you," Liya replied.

"You're going to go to Mommy for a bit, okay?" Wren said to Illa and he handed her back to Liya. Illa pouted slightly and Wren smiled at her. "It's just for a bit, okay? I just have to—"

"Wren, she's one. You don't have to explain to her in so much detail," Liya pointed out.

Wren laughed and then focused his attention on Sutton. "Come on. Let me show you."

Wren and Sutton disappeared down the hallway to the guestroom, and left Liya standing there with Illa and the four others. It was strange—they didn't say a word, or even look her directly in the eyes.

Wolf's Baby 83

"Are you guys not allowed to speak to me?" she asked.

"We're just the brawn," Krew said in a really deep voice that didn't surprise Liya at all. "We're not here to make polite conversation."

"I'm sure that's not true," Liya said with a half smile. "Can I get you guys anything to drink, or to eat?"

The four glanced at one another and Ash stepped forward. "Requesting permission for a cup of coffee, ma'am."

"Gosh, don't call me ma'am. That's my mother," Liya scoffed and walked to the kitchen. "Come on, you guys."

She had the four guys sit at the kitchen table, made them coffee and set out a plate of cookies, which they devoured in a matter of seconds. They were like four little boys, eating cookies and making jokes.

A few minutes later, Liya saw Wren and Sutton enter the kitchen and Sutton frowned at the four Zetas.

"What's all this?" Sutton asked sternly.

"Well, if they're going to be watching the house, I don't want them to get hungry in the process," Liya answered.

Sutton looked at Wren, who simply shrugged his shoulders. Sutton huffed and shook his head. "Alright, teatime is over. Ash, you take the east. Krew, you're on the west point. Jace, you're in the front of the house with me, and Torin, you're at the back."

"Yes, Sutton," the four of them muttered and stood from the table.

Krew turned to Liya, handed Illa back to her and smiled slightly. "Thank you, Liya."

"You're welcome," she said with a nod.

Sutton shook his head and followed them outside.

Liya looked at Wren apologetically. "I'm sorry, I didn't want to get them in trouble."

"You don't have to apologize. You're the lady of the house now. You can do whatever you want."

"Is that so?" she asked and raised her eyebrows. "Because I've been thinking about moving some of the furniture around."

"Whatever you want."

She narrowed her eyes slightly and nodded. "I'm kidding. So, anyway, Sutton isn't going to punish them or anything?"

"Because you gave them cookies and coffee? No."

"He looked really angry," Liya said.

"Sutton needs to relax, so don't even worry about it," Wren suggested. "Besides, you treated them well, so they'll make sure that no one comes remotely close to this house."

"That's good to know," she responded. "Are all Zetas bodyguards?"

"Not all of them, no. These guys are four brothers, so they're bound by more than the moon."

"Family loyalty," Liya said simply and glanced at Wren, whose jaw clenched. "Hey," she said, and he looked at her. "We're your family now, okay?"

Wren nodded simply and placed his hand on her shoulder. "You're my family now."

About an hour later, Wren and Liya lay on his bed, with Illa lying between them, drinking her bottle.

"I have a confession to make," he whispered.

Liya glanced at him and pouted slightly. "What's that?"

"Before I met you and Illa, I never thought that I would ever want to have kids," he said. "I think I had this fear that I would turn out just like my father, and that kind of made me avoid it at all costs."

"You're not your father, Wren, and you're great with her. She totally loves you."

"Well, I love her, too."

Liya smiled and looked at him. She had never found him as sexy as she found him at that very moment. He lay on his side, his head resting on his pillow, and his hand rubbing Illa's stomach. Even though he had never thought that he would ever be a good father, he was totally Daddy-material at that moment, and every other moment he spent with Illa. It definitely lit a fire in all the right places in Liya's body, and if their lives weren't in danger, and if Illa wasn't lying in between them, she'd definitely be calling *him* 'Daddy'. A smile formed on her lips and he looked at her with a grin, as if he knew exactly what she was thinking.

"You shouldn't look at me like that, you know," he said in a low and sexy tone.

"Why not?" she asked with a pout.

"Because I might just have to tell Krew to take Illa for an hour," he said with a wink.

Liya giggled softly. "I don't know what you mean," she said innocently.

"What I would do to you if I could," he whispered.

"Tell me," she whispered back and raised an intrigued eyebrow at him.

He asked hesitantly, "With Illa here?"

"She's asleep," Liya said and looked at Illa beside her.

"Simple. I'd just rip all your clothes off and make you feel things you've never felt before," he answered.

"Wow, you don't waste any time, do you?" Liya gasped.

Wren smirked and wiggled his eyebrows suggestively, making Liya giggle quietly.

"I'm not even touching you and I'm all fired up," Wren whispered.

"Same here," Liya said and looked down at her feet. "Wren, I'm sorry for dragging you into this whole mess. I never wanted to involve anyone in this. I just want to be safe, and Illa to be safe."

"You're kind of ruining the mood here," he said.

"I know, but I'm serious. I know you didn't exactly sign up for this, but thank you. I don't really have the words to express how much I appreciate you."

Wren reached over and brushed a strand of blonde hair off her face, tucking it behind her ear. "You're welcome, and you didn't drag me into anything. I could have said no. I could have driven away when you hit my car. I could have chased you out of my house when I saw your tattoo, but I didn't. Not only because we imprinted but because I chose to. I chose to be a part of this, and if I could go back and do it all over again, I'd choose the same path. Over and over again."

Liya smiled and glanced at Illa, watching her little chest move up and down as she breathed peacefully. Liya would never tire of looking at her daughter sleeping, and she remembered when Illa was a newborn, she would spend most of her nights and days looking at her sleeping baby with a heart filled with love. It didn't matter if she was tired from the lack of sleep associated with being a new mother. Liya loved every moment of it, and even Hunter backed off from her for that while, which she was grateful for. She had never considered having a baby, but it was something that happened, and she was happy about it. Now Liya could not imagine her life without little Illa.

"Can I ask you something?" Wren asked after a brief silence.

Liya tore her gaze away from Illa and glanced at him. "Of course. You can always ask me anything."

"How did you know you were ready to have kids?" Wren asked.

"I don't think we're ever really ready," she answered. "Illa wasn't planned, but she's definitely the best thing that ever happened to me."

"Even if she's Hunter's daughter?"

"She's my daughter too, so she's half of me. Her father

Wolf's Baby 87

doesn't define who she is, and who she's going to become," Liya whispered and looked at him.

He nodded slowly and glanced down at Illa. "She's going to be great one day."

Liya smiled and looked at Wren. "She already is."

Wren took her hand and smiled slightly. "So are you, Liya."

8

Wren stepped onto the snowy path that led through the forested area behind Liya's house to her back door, and surveyed the area around him.

The conversation he had had with her about his father and Cole still lingered in his mind, and he just couldn't stop thinking about it.

Frankly, Wren wouldn't be surprised if Cole had gotten himself involved in Crescent activities. Cole had never been the type of person who could differentiate from right or wrong, and he'd often do things without considering his family, or the pack. He'd do whatever he wanted, and for some reason Luther always seemed to tolerate and accept what he did. Even if it was the worst thing imaginable.

Wren remembered the time when Cole accidentally tipped over the rowboat in which he and one of his many human girl-friends spent the day. She got stuck under the overturned boat and tragically drowned. Luther didn't shout or do anything to Cole, but instead gave a lecture to the rest of the family that they weren't meant to keep human company, not even as pets.

Wren shivered as he thought of Cole's possible involvement

with the Crescents and possibly trying to recruit them into their pack, but the thought that Luther could have also known about it, and condoned it, was what made Wren feel sick to his stomach. He never thought his father would ever have anything to do with the Crescents after what happened. On more than one occasion did the Wylde family appear on the Crescents' radar, but it wasn't because of their indiscretions. Maybe the Crescents found them too boring and wanted to spice things up a bit. Little did they know that there were plenty of things happening in their family that they were not even allowed to talk about with one another.

Wren kicked the snow in front of him as he clenched his jaw, flashbacks of his past rushing back. He hated reliving his memories, as if experiencing them the first time wasn't bad enough.

Branches cracked and he jumped slightly, feeling much more on edge than he should. Something was wrong, but he couldn't put his finger on it. He tried to think of something more pleasant and the image of Liya on his kitchen table filled his mind, creating an uncomfortable shift in his jeans.

"For heaven's sake," he muttered as he adjusted himself.

Now was not the time to think about Liya naked on the kitchen table with her legs wrapped around him. The heat rose inside him again and he shook his head.

"Wren, pull it together," he muttered again as he found himself at her back porch. He climbed up the three stairs and stopped a few inches from the door.

As he opened the back door, he checked around him one more time before stepping inside. The inside was immaculately cleaned thanks to Luca and his cleaning crew, and Wren made his way through the house. He wasn't sure what he was looking for, but at the moment, anything would be better than nothing. He knew he might also be looking for something that wasn't even there, but it was worth a try.

He went upstairs and searched the small loft area. There wasn't much in there, but he opened the large chest of drawers, rummaging inside. There was nothing that belonged to Liya, and he clenched his fists in frustration.

Liya's words from earlier kept replaying in his mind and he was once again reminded that he wasn't like his father. That was probably one of the things that he had struggled with the most in his life. He didn't *ever* want to turn into his father, but he was so afraid that he would, so he built high, impenetrable walls around him which no one was able to get through.

Except for Liya.

She managed to swat them away as if they were made of paper. She made him open up about his family, and about himself, and she even made him cry. He recalled Luther scolding him when he cried during his younger years, calling him weak, but Liya insisted that it didn't make him any less of a man. In fact, she was convinced it showed true strength. Wren still struggled with the idea of showing his emotions and emotionally connecting with others. It had been easy with Liya and Illa, but Wren didn't know if he'd ever be ready to open up to the rest of the world.

The floorboards creaked from downstairs, and Wren turned around and noticed a shadow quickly moving out of sight. He quietly descended the stairs, and as he rounded the corner, he saw someone in the kitchen.

"Who the hell are you?" Wren said.

The guy, who was about as tall as Wren, with dark hair and broad shoulders, turned around, and judging by the look on his face, he was pissed beyond belief.

The familiar scent filled Wren's nostrils and he narrowed his eyes. "You're Hunter."

"And you must be..." He paused and pretended to think for a second. "Oh yeah, I don't care."

Wolf's Baby   91

"I'm Wren."

Hunter glanced at him with haughty derision. "I know who you are, but as I said, I don't care."

"What are you doing here?" Wren asked.

"I could ask you that same question," Hunter answered and turned to him.

"Look I don't know why you're in Bigfork terrorizing Liya, but it's got to stop," Wren said, mentally preparing himself for a sudden attack. From what he had heard about Hunter, he wasn't going to take any chances.

"She burnt down my goddamn house, but I'm the one whose terrorizing her," Hunter scoffed incredulously. "What about my feelings?"

"From what I heard, you don't have any," Wren said simply.

"For an Alpha, you're pretty clueless," Hunter muttered and when Wren growled at him angrily, baring his teeth, he held his hands up in defeat. "Relax, that was a joke."

"I'm going to ask you again, and it will be the last time," Wren said and stepped towards Hunter. "What are you doing here?"

"I thought my little message was quite clear last night," Hunter answered casually.

Even though he seemed composed, Wren kept his defenses up and at the ready. "Relax, dude. I'm not here for you, or Liya. I just want my daughter," Hunter shrugged.

"No," Wren answered simply.

Hunter frowned and crossed his arms. "It wasn't a request. She's mine."

"You can't have her. So you can just go on home now," Wren said.

Hunter chuckled and shook his head. "You don't understand. I need her. She's got an amazing calming ability that might grow into more, and—"

"So that's the only reason you want her back?" Wren asked in disgust. "Because of her ability? Not because she's your daughter?"

"She's a Crescent, and so is Liya," Hunter said and took another step closer to him. "You *do* know that, right?"

"They're not anymore. They're a part of *my* pack now," Wren answered and pushed his chest out to show his dominance.

"Oh, right. Because of the imprinting thing?" Hunter asked. "How is that, by the way? Can you not keep your hands off each other or what?"

Wren looked at him with contempt and refused to answer.

"Oh, come on. Stop being so damn stuck-up. What's it to you if I take Illa? She's not your daughter," Hunter said and with his thumbs clenched inside his fists.

"It doesn't matter. Liya is mine now and that makes Illa mine too, and I am *not* going to allow anyone to take either of them away without a fight," Wren answered.

"Why are Alphas always so eager to fight?" Hunter asked, unfazed by Wren's threats.

"Because we protect what is ours," Wren hissed.

"*Yours.*" Hunter smirked in amusement and said, "Wow, I never thought Liya would finally find someone to imprint with again."

"What do you mean, *again*?" Wren asked with narrowed eyes and Hunter laughed wickedly.

"I knew there was *something* she wasn't telling you. She didn't tell me either. I had to find out from my best friend," Hunter said with a bitter chuckle.

"Am I supposed to feel sorry for you?" Wren asked.

"No. I don't want your sympathy," Hunter answered. "I'm the one who should feel sorry for you, really. Your new girlfriend is keeping secrets from you. Dangerous secrets."

"Why should I listen to you? I don't know you," Wren said.

"That may be true, but you should know who you've imprinted on. She's keeping things from you that are kind of important, wouldn't you say? That's not a good way to start a relationship," Hunter pointed out as he slowly started to circle Wren.

"What the hell do you know about good relationships?" Wren growled.

"Let me guess, Liya told you I was abusive and pushed her around," Hunter said.

"She showed me her scars, and not just the ones on her skin," Wren answered.

"That's very noble of you, to save the little damsel in distress," Hunter sneered. "You should just remember that we all carry around secrets of our own. Secrets we don't tell anyone, whether we imprinted on them or not."

"If you have something to say to me, then just say it," Wren grumbled.

Hunter sneered at him. "Liya hasn't told you about Miles, has she?"

"Who the hell is Miles?"

"Maybe I should let her tell you instead. It's not my place, and it's not my story to tell. I'm just here to warn you," Hunter said.

"I can look after myself," Wren muttered.

"I can see that. You've grown up a lot since the last time I saw you."

Wren stepped forward. "What the hell is *that* supposed to mean? When did you see me?"

"My folks lived out in Silver Bay around the fifties, too," Hunter said.

"You're lying," Wren scowled.

"Why would I do that?"

"You're a Crescent, and Crescents lie."

"Then Liya is true to her pack after all," Hunter smirked. "I'll see you around, Wren."

"Wait," Wren growled, and Hunter glanced at him expectantly. "You knew my family?"

"Everyone knew your family, Wren," Hunter answered simply. "Now you go home and ask Liya to tell you all about Miles."

Hunter walked past Wren and Wren suddenly grabbed his arm. "You're going to leave Bigfork, right now. I don't ever want to see you here again."

"Watch that temper, Alpha," Hunter growled. "I'm just here for Illa."

Wren's grasp tightened and he growled as well. "Just go back to wherever the hell it is that you came from."

"As I said, I'm not here to fight," Hunter said and held his hands up in the air.

Wren narrowed his eyes and his grip loosened. He wasn't sure what he thought when Hunter stepped away and quietly left the house, but standing there by himself in the center of the room, he began to question everything that had happened in the last few weeks.

Was Hunter telling the truth? Had Liya imprinted before? If she had, it would be impossible for her to imprint again. Wolves mated for life, and even after one dies, they're unable to imprint again, right?

There were too many questions floating around in Wren's mind, but there was only one way to find out.

He had to ask Liya.

Wren arrived home about an hour later, having gone for a drive to try to clear his head. The new information Hunter had brought to light was troubling to Wren, and worst of all, it may or may not have even been true. Dissatisfied that his head was still as much a mess as it was when he left Liya's house, he stepped into the living room to find Liya on the floor, playing with Illa. Illa chased after a fluffy pink ball and laughed every time she threw it back to Liya.

"Hey, you," Liya said as she smiled up at him. "We were wondering where you've been."

Wren approached them and crouched down beside Illa. "Hey. I just had to do a few things in town."

"Is everything okay?" she asked, and he studied her. Her blue eyes looked worried, but he wasn't in the right frame of mind to talk to her just yet.

Usually, Wren would deal with his problems or any issue that arose by himself initially. He'd let it fester in his mind, more often than not exaggerating it tremendously and unnecessarily. He had the tendency to make a mountain out of a molehill, and he wasn't sure how to not do it. It had been the way he dealt with things ever since he could remember, and too much time had passed by for him to change his ways.

"Wren?" she asked with a frown and Wren realized he didn't answer her.

"Yeah," he shrugged and stood up.

"Are you sure?" she asked. "You have that look on your face again."

"Now you're an expert on reading my facial expressions," he grumbled as he walked to the kitchen.

Liya pushed herself up from the floor and walked towards him. "What is going on?"

"Nothing, okay? Can you just let it go?" Wren asked with a slight scowl.

Liya took a step back and he looked at her, his eyes flashing. "I'm sorry," she said and held her hands up in defeat. "I don't want to fight with you."

Wren looked at her and the anger built up inside him at a steady pace. Hunter's words repeated in his mind and he couldn't look at Liya anymore. He lowered his gaze and shook his head.

"Just tell me what's wrong. Maybe I can help."

"I saw Hunter," Wren said simply.

Liya's eyes widened and she stepped forward again. "When? Where?"

"It doesn't matter," Wren muttered.

"Of course it does. Are you okay? Did he do anything to you?" she asked, and Wren shook his head again. "Oh, no. Did you fight with him? Is he dead?"

"No. He knew my family," Wren answered, not moving his gaze from her.

"Oh," she answered flatly, not really knowing how to respond to that. "Is that a good thing?"

"You tell me, Liya," Wren said and crinkled his nose.

"What are you talking about?" she asked.

"Tell me about Miles."

Liya stood frozen on the spot, her eyes fixed on him. She let out a breath and said, "Hunter told you about Miles?"

"Partly, but he said I should ask you."

"Wren, listen to me—" she said but he cut her off by raising his hand.

"You already imprinted," he asked, "with this Miles person?"

"Yes, but—"

"Why didn't you tell me?" Wren demanded, his tone getting louder with every word he said.

"Because I didn't think it mattered," she answered.

Wren's blood boiled in his veins and he exploded. "How could it not matter? Did you only pretend to imprint with me?"

"No, of course not. I—"

"Then what, Liya? You can't imprint twice!" he exclaimed.

"Miles died, okay? Is that what you wanted to hear?" Liya asked.

Wren bit down on his bottom lip and shook his head at himself.

"Miles was killed by a Crescent, and yes, I *did* love him. Yes, he was a big part of my life, and yes, I will always think about him because that bond isn't just broken by death, okay? I should have told you, sure, but it's painful. You should know all about it. I spent so much time not pressing you to tell me things that you don't feel comfortable talking about. I *never* put pressure on you to do anything you weren't ready for. I thought that you'd extend the same courtesy to me, but clearly I was wrong," Liya said and turned away.

"Liya, wait..." Wren said, wanting her to come back to him, but she walked to Illa, picked her up and stomped down the hallway.

"Liya, please," Wren called after her, but she ignored him completely.

Within a few minutes, Liya came back down the hallway with her and Illa's bags, and Wren's heart sank into his boots.

"Where are you going?"

"Anywhere but here," she muttered as she sat Illa on the couch and put her jacket on.

"It's freezing outside. Your car isn't even here. You can't walk home," he pointed out.

"I called Krew. He'll be here in a few minutes to take us home," Liya answered as she picked Illa up from the couch.

"You really don't have to go," Wren said and approached her.

"No, I think I do. I've clearly overstayed my welcome, so we'll just go," Liya said and they heard a car pull up outside, followed by a knock on the door. "That's Krew."

"What about Hunter? What if he hurts you and takes Illa away?" Wren asked as Liya walked to the door.

Liya stopped in front of the door, her hand resting on the

doorknob. She glanced at him over her shoulder and said snidely, "Well, then that's on *your* conscience, Wren."

Liya opened the door and Krew stood on the front porch.

"Are you ready?" Krew asked.

"Yeah, can you just get our bags, please?" Liya asked, as she and Illa walked to Krew's SUV and climbed inside without a word.

"Of course," Krew answered and stepped into the house.

Wren watched as he took the bags, and as he was about to leave the house, Wren stepped in front of him.

"Step aside, Wren," Krew said calmly.

Wren's nostrils flared and he hissed, "I am your Alpha, Krew, and you do not defy me."

"It's one thing to defy you, but it is an entirely different thing to defy the Alpha's mate. You should know that. She takes precedence, especially with little Illa, but you know this," Krew said, reminding Wren of the rules surrounding the mate of the Alpha.

When he was a young pup, Wren had noticed a few things about how his father treated his mother when it came to making decisions, especially when it came to their sons. He often thought that the Alpha had the final say in everything. With matters relating to the pack in general, the Alpha was in charge. In fact, if he wasn't imprinted at the time, he was in charge of everything.

After an Alpha imprinted, however, all that changed. The Alpha still had a firm grasp on being in charge, but for any issue involving the safety of himself, his mate, or their children, biological or not, he was not. It was down to the mate to have the final say. That was exactly why Skye had been the one who would have the final say when it related to anything about their five sons and their safety.

Wren completely forgot about that, as he was convinced he'd never imprint willingly, although he should have realized that imprinting wasn't a choice of will. Now that he had imprinted with Liya, she now had the final say where her own and Illa's safety was concerned, although Wren thought that she *was* being a little overly dramatic. Then again, he *did* accuse her of pretending to imprint on him and lying to him about something that she wasn't ready to tell him, and went off on her because he felt insecure about himself. Wren bit his bottom lip and silently scolded himself.

"She asked for my help, Wren, and I am going to do whatever she asks, not to defy you, but to protect her. That's what us Zetas do. If you can't handle that, take it up with her. I'm not going to be the one who tells her that she has to stay here. I have no idea what she is capable of."

"You're *afraid* of her," Wren said and creased his brow.

"Respect is often mistaken for fear, Wren, although most don't know the difference," Krew said simply and he looked at Wren expectantly. "Now step aside, please."

Wren nodded. He knew there was nothing he could do to stop Liya from leaving, or Krew from taking her away, so instead of defying his own rules, he stepped aside. He watched as Krew left the house and Wren stood in the doorway as the SUV drove off, taking his entire life away from him.

It was *his* fault, he knew this, but if he tried to stop her from leaving, it would only end up in a fight, and the last thing he wanted was to fight with her.

He would fight *for* her, he just wasn't sure how.

He tried to think back to a time where Skye got upset with Luther and how Luther handled it, but he came up short.

"I don't know what to do," he muttered as he closed the door behind him and leaned his back against the door.

A strange feeling washed over him as he thought back to the time when he and River were cornered by a hostile pack passing through town. He also remembered seeing Skye transform from a timid, nature-loving woman into a vicious and ferocious wolf who was ready to slaughter an entire pack to ensure the safety of her two children. Wren had never seen his mother in that way before, and found it interesting when the entire hostile pack ran for the hills when they figured out Skye was the mate of the Alpha. He had never seen a pack of wolves cower in fear the way that pack did. From that moment on he knew that there was nothing stronger than a mother's love. Skye would have fought to the death for her children, and sadly, she ultimately did.

A sudden knock on the front door made him jump and he realized that his defenses were completely down and his senses were lacking. Normally he would know if someone was outside his house even before they climbed out of their car.

Was this Liya's doing? Did she take a part of him when she left?

There was another knock on the door and he shook his head, getting rid of the foolish thoughts in his mind. He opened the door to see Sutton standing in the doorway.

Wren sighed, clenched his jaw and stepped aside, allowing Sutton to enter.

Sutton glanced at him with a scowl. "What's going on?"

"Nothing," Wren muttered and turned away.

"Wren, I just saw Krew's car drive off with Liya and Illa in the back seat. Clearly *something* is going on," Sutton pointed out.

"I don't want to talk about it," Wren grumbled.

"For God's sake, Wren. You have to talk about it sometime. In fact, I'm really worried about the fact that you don't talk at all, because one of these days you're going to explode and there are going to be a lot of casualties who get caught in the blast, yourself included," Sutton said as he stepped forward. "I don't want that to happen."

Wren sighed but still didn't say a word. He simply glowered, staring out in front of him.

"Wren, please. Talk to me," Sutton said. "I'm your Beta, but I'm also your friend."

Wren glanced at him with a frown and asked, "I'm your friend?"

"Of course. I'd do anything for you. I thought you knew that."

"I do know that, I just didn't think that you considered me as a friend," Wren said.

Sutton smiled slightly and placed his hand on Wren's shoulder. "You're my friend and I'm yours, Wren. Nothing is going to change that. Okay?" When Wren nodded, Sutton asked again, "Now, what's going on?"

"I stopped by Liya's house yesterday, and Hunter was there," he explained.

"Hunter, as in Liya's ex-boyfriend, the psycho, abusive Crescent hunter?" Sutton asked in disbelief.

"Yeah. How do you know him?"

"Most people do. He's dangerous. Did he try to attack you?"

"No, he was fine. He wasn't there to fight, or that's what he told me," Wren said. "He didn't seem at all like the monster Liya described to me."

"You don't believe her?" Sutton asked. "Because I can back up her stories. He's a terrible person, but loyal to those Crescents. He'll do whatever they ask him to, no questions asked."

"What hold do they have over him?" Wren asked.

"He was born a Crescent; he grew up forced to watch his father mentally and physically torture his mother for fun. He's had a troubled life filled with aggression and pain, and having the abilities he has, the Alpha and Betas took him in after his father was punished for ultimately killing his mother, who was the daughter of the Alpha."

"He's the grandson of the Crescent Alpha?" Wren exclaimed,

and Sutton nodded. "Holy shit. No wonder no one believed her. He's practically untouchable."

"Exactly," Sutton said and dug his hands into the front pockets of his jeans.

"I *hate* those damn Crescents."

"For all the normal reasons?"

Wren glanced at Sutton hesitantly and shook his head. "For reasons I've never talked about to anyone, except Liya," he said, and Sutton looked at him with wide eyes. "The Crescents found it amusing to mess up my family's lives on more than one occasion. They forced us to leave our homes many times, and we had to start over every single time. The last time, we moved back to our old hometown of Silver Bay in Minnesota. My mom loved that house so much, and it made me happy to see her happy. I was a real Momma's boy, apparently."

"That *is* surprising. I can't imagine you being close to anybody," Sutton scoffed.

"One night we woke up and our house was in flames. My brothers and I got out, but my parents didn't," Wren said and he watched as Sutton's face paled. "We never really found out who did it, but I've always known it was them. The Crescents. They wanted us gone for good, but they slipped up. They left us alive."

Sutton let out a heavy sigh, shaking his head in disbelief. "Wren, I'm so sorry. What happened to your brothers?"

"We all went our separate ways because we couldn't agree on anything. I haven't seen them or heard of them since then, and I don't want to either. If they don't want to make contact with me, then I don't want to make contact with them."

"And you all inherited your stubbornness from your father, right?" Sutton asked wryly.

"I guess you can say that, yes," Wren said and smiled slightly.

"I'm sorry, Wren. I didn't know."

"Of course you didn't know. I never told anyone about it. I

just didn't want to think about it, but when Liya came into town and she brought all her baggage along, it just took me back to that time where I was angry and resentful. She made it all better, though. She scratched off the surface that I so desperately wanted to keep covered and aired it out. She brought it out into the open and she changed everything. She changed me, she made me better," Wren said and lowered his head miserably.

"What are you going to do?"

"I messed up, big time."

"I kind of gathered that, since she left. Did she go back to her house?" Sutton asked, and Wren nodded. "What if Hunter is there? Are you *really* going to allow him to take Illa?"

"I'll kill him with my bare hands if he even touches a hair on either of their heads," Wren growled.

"Good, but save your aggression for Hunter," Sutton said.

"She won't let me near her or Illa right now. She's pissed," Wren scowled, "and I don't even blame her."

"What did you do, by the way?" Sutton asked.

"I believed Hunter and not her."

Sutton cringed painfully and shook his head. "You do realize you'll be hearing about this for the rest of your life after all this crap is over, right?"

"As long as she's there to give me crap about it, I don't mind."

Sutton grinned. "It's weird to see you like this. As long as I've known you, you've never opened up to me before, or to anyone. It's kind of nice, but it's also kind of terrifying."

"You're telling me," Wren scoffed. "Sutton, could you do me a favor?"

"Sure, anything," he answered.

"Could you go see if she is okay?" Wren asked and glared at Sutton, who seemed unfazed by Wren's impatient tone.

"She's not going to let me in," Sutton answered.

"I know, but you could just check on her without her knowing it."

"I'm not going to spy on your woman, Wren," Sutton said as he walked away.

"Please," Wren said, his tone desperate.

Sutton pursed his lips and nodded. "Okay. I'll do it."

'Thank you," Wren said gratefully.

"I just have a few things to do for Ruby, and then I'll check in on Liya," Sutton said.

Ruby was Sutton's wife who recently found out she was expecting their first baby. It was an exciting time for them, but Wren knew that Sutton was as nervous as they came, even though he denied it with his life. Wren knew much more about Sutton than anyone, as Sutton was his only Beta, his second in command. Wren had not trusted anyone else to be a Beta, and he knew that he could rely on Sutton no matter what. Wren was convinced that if he asked Sutton to walk through Hell with him, Sutton wouldn't question him and would follow him without argument.

"Give my regards to Ruby," Wren said. "How is she, by the way?"

"Pregnancy doesn't seem to agree with her. She's been really moody. Probably all those hormones," Sutton said. "Who knows how the human race works, right?"

"Yeah, she's probably the only one who is decent and doesn't want to kill us," Wren said.

"Maybe," Sutton said and chuckled. "I'll give you a call later."

Wren nodded and watched as Sutton left the house. He shivered as the emptiness and the quiet inside his house enveloped him. Over the past few weeks he had grown accustomed to the noisiness that went with having a woman and a one-year-old baby in the house. Now there was nothing but silence and cold. He sat down on the couch and suddenly realized how exhausted he was. He felt drained and tired, and lay back against the soft pillow. Liya's scent still lingered in the house, especially on the pillow, and he scolded himself once again. He closed his eyes for a second, and before he could stop himself, he fell into an exhausted yet peaceful slumber.

9

—————

Deep down, Liya was terrified to be back at the house, but she was too proud, and stubborn, to admit it. She was also hurt by Wren and his pathetic accusations. She couldn't understand why he would believe Hunter instead of believing her.

Illa, of course, was more than happy to be out of the car and crawled happily along the carpets on her own little mission to retrieve the pink and blue ball she threw around the living room while Liya made dinner.

After Liya and Illa took a bath and were snugly dressed in their warm pajamas, they went to bed, but Liya couldn't fall asleep. She was exhausted, feeling drained for some reason, but even after the hundredth attempt to fall asleep, she glanced over at Illa and shook her head with envy. At most times, Liya wished she could fall asleep as easily as Illa could. Liya slowly climbed out of bed, careful not to wake Illa, although Illa could sleep through most things, and walked down the hallway to the kitchen. She opened the refrigerator and rummaged through it, looking for something to snack on. She heard the floorboards creak behind her and she spun around. A pair of glowing yellow eyes watched her from the shadows and she didn't even have to guess who it was. She already knew. She always knew.

"Liya," Hunter said as he stepped out from the shadows and slowly approached her.

"What are you doing here?" she asked as she slowly reached for the handle of the knife drawer.

"Oh, I thought you got my note," he said with an unwarranted smile and long, drawn-out blinks.

"The one on the brick that you threw through a window right were Illa slept?" Liya asked. "You could have seriously hurt her; you know that?"

"It wasn't my intention to hurt her, Liya, or you."

"That is bullshit. You spent nearly every night beating on me, telling me how worthless I was and that I was lucky to have someone like you who could guide me to be the right kind of Crescent, because according to your pathetic excuse of a pack, *I* was the problem," she whispered as she slid her hand into the half-open drawer and reached for a knife.

"I wouldn't do that if I were you," he warned. "I'm much stronger than you are, and you know it."

In a sudden move, Hunter swooped in on her, grabbed her by the shoulders and pushed her up against the wall.

"If you want to kill me, just do it, but you're not getting anywhere near Illa," she growled.

"And who's going to stop me? You?" he asked with a smirk.

Before she could answer, he threw her across the room and she crashed into a small end table, landing on the ground.

A pain shot through her shoulder and she groaned. As she rolled onto her back, Hunter stood over her and laughed wickedly.

"Do you seriously think that you can stop me from taking what I want? You were never able to, and you never will. All that you're good at is running and hiding," he said as he crouched beside her and wrapped his hands around her throat. "But you're not nearly as good a hider as I am a tracker."

"Please don't do this," Liya begged, gasping for breath.

"You burnt down my house, Liya. You took my daughter away from me. You'll be lucky if you make it out alive," he snarled as he slammed her head into the ground.

The world spun hazily around Liya as she tried to regain her sense of self, trying to fight back, but she couldn't. She *did, however,* realize that Hunter's hands were no longer at her throat, but it still did not make her breathing any easier.

"Hunter," she called out as she pushed herself up onto her knees. She felt the blood trickle down from her temple and lightly touched it. The sight of her own blood had little effect on her, but the thought that Hunter would soon find Illa in the bedroom caused waves of nausea to rise up inside her.

"Don't you dare, Hunter!"

"Or what, Liya? Is your Alpha boyfriend coming for me? I don't think so, because he's scared of me, and he should be. If he comes after me, we'll come after him, again. We'll finish him off just like we planned on doing in the fifties," Hunter smiled wickedly.

"It was you?" she gasped. "You burnt down their house? You killed his parents?"

"United they were strong, having all those abilities. They didn't want to share them, so we had to get rid of them. All of them. Only we didn't."

"You're not going to get away with this."

"Maybe not, or maybe I am," he shrugged nonchalantly and made his way down the hallway. Her blood ran cold in her veins as she heard Illa's little cries from the bedroom and she yelled out his name again a few times.

To her horror, she saw Hunter walk down the hallway towards her, holding Illa in his arms.

Wolf's Baby

"No, please. Hunter, don't do this. She's my daughter, too," Liya pleaded as hot tears stung her eyes and she reached out her hands to him. "Please give her to me."

"This is on you," Hunter said

"No, no, please don't take her," Liya begged.

Hunter, unfazed by Liya's words, stepped over her and walked to the door. Illa looked at Liya over her father's shoulder and waved at Liya, unaware of what was happening.

"My baby!" Liya cried out.

Hunter stopped at the door. "It was really nice seeing you, Liya."

Liya yelled out his name, still unable to stand up, and crawled to the door. She sobbed with every breath she took and finally collapsed in a pile on the floor in front of the door.

Liya woke to a pounding sound, and at first, she thought it was her head. The smell of her blood had faded slightly, and she allowed her eyes to focus. The pounding continued, and she realized it wasn't coming from her head at all.

"Liya! Open the door!"

Who is that? she thought and tried to push herself up, but her arms were powerless, and she could only lie helpless on the floor.

A loud crash echoed through her ears as the door flew open and the sound tore through her skull so badly she shut her eyes and winced painfully.

"Liya, are you okay?"

Liya opened her eyes and looked up into the deep green eyes of Sutton, who was crouched down beside her, panic and concern in his eyes.

"Are you okay?" he asked again and she frowned.

"What are you doing here?" she asked weakly.

"I came to check if you were okay, and I saw Hunter speeding off in his car," Sutton answered. "Are you hurt?"

"My head hurts," she muttered, and he helped her up from the floor and sat her down on the couch.

"It looks like you got hit pretty hard," Sutton said as he walked to the freezer, opened it and took out a bag of frozen peas. "Here," he said as he handed it to her.

"Thanks," she groaned and closed her eyes for a second.

Sutton sat down beside her and asked, "Did Hunter take Illa?"

Liya opened her eyes and they immediately filled with tears. "He did. I couldn't stop him. He took my baby and I couldn't even stop him," she said in between sobs.

"It's okay. We'll get her back."

"I don't even know where they went," she said.

"I do," a voice came from the door and Liya glanced over her shoulder. Her jaw clenched as she stood from the couch, even though Sutton insisted that she sit down. She pressed her bag of peas against her temple and glared at Wren. She was still so angry at him, but she couldn't stop the tears from running down her cheeks.

"What are you doing here?" Liya asked through her tears.

"I came here to help you get Illa back,"

"I don't need your help," she said as she turned away.

The world spun around her violently and her legs gave way under her. Wren caught her and placed her back on the couch.

"You're just as stubborn as me," Wren muttered.

"That's true," Sutton said behind them, which made the corners of Wren's mouth curl up slightly.

Liya glanced at him and winced. "I don't know if I'm more angry or relieved to see you."

"She hit her head pretty hard," Sutton said again.

"I can hear you, you know," Liya muttered. "Why?"

"Why what? Why am I here?" he asked and brushed a lock

of hair from her face. "I told you. I want to get Illa back as much as you want to."

"Why?"

"Because she's my family, and so are you. I love you both more than I can ever describe," he answered.

"You have a strange way of showing it," she said and looked at him with haughty derision.

"I'm trying, okay? This is really hard for me. I've never been someone to just admit when they're wrong, or that someone else means more to me than I do," Wren answered.

"It's true, you know," Sutton said from the other side of the room.

Liya placed her palm against Wren's cheek.

"And I'm sorry that I doubted you. I know how that feels, and while there is no excuse for what I did, I hope you can forgive me, because I've never loved anyone the way I love you and Illa."

"He hasn't," Sutton said again.

Wren narrowed his eyes in agitation while looking in Sutton's direction. "Could you maybe call Luca, outside, please? Like, now?"

"Sure," Sutton said and left the house.

"You didn't have to be mean to him," Liya muttered and Wren scoffed. "Why is he calling Luca?"

"Well, Luca is a Delta, a healer, and he can take care of that wound for you," Wren explained.

"Wren, I don't want to sound disrespectful or ungrateful, but there's no time for all that. We have to find Illa."

"I know exactly where they are. I have his scent memorized in my mind."

"After all this time?" she asked.

"What do you mean all this time?" Wren asked with a deep and troubling grimaced expression.

"Wren?" Luca said behind them and Wren glanced over his shoulder at Luca and Sutton standing in the doorway.

"Hey, Luca. Thanks for coming," Wren said. "Come on in."

"I came as soon as I could," Luca said. "I heard what happened. Are you okay, Liya?"

"I'm bleeding, I might be concussed, and my abusive ex-boyfriend kidnapped my daughter. How do you think I'm doing?"

"Well, I can take care of the first two for you," Luca said and crouched down beside her. "Let me take a look at that."

Liya lowered the bag of peas and Luca briefly examined her head and placed his hand against her temple. She winced painfully.

"It's okay. This is just going to sting a little, but it will only be for a second or two, okay?" Luca said and Liya nodded.

Liya felt a current radiate into her and the heat traveled to her temple. As it started to sting, she closed her eyes, and a shiver ran down her spine. For a moment it felt as though she was submerged under hot water, floating along without direction or reason. The pain started to subside, and the heat completely disappeared. She slowly opened her eyes and looked at Luca.

He raised his eyebrows expectantly and asked, "How do you feel?"

Liya frowned slightly, and it felt strange not to feel any pain after the waves of torment that had ripped through her skull for the last hour. "I feel great, actually. How did you do that?"

"It's just something that I do," Luca said warmly.

"Thank you," she said and hugged him.

"You're welcome," he said awkwardly.

Liya stood up from the couch and approached Wren. "So, Alpha, what do we do now?"

"Hold on. You said something about remembering Hunter's scent after all this time," Wren said.

Liya shifted her weight uncomfortably and placed her hands on her hips.

"What is it?" he asked and gave Luca and Sutton a dismissive wave.

Liya glanced at Luca and Sutton leaving and took a deep breath. "Hunter told me that it was him and a few Crescents who were the ones who..." Her voice trailed off and she took another breath as Wren looked at her expectantly. "They were the ones who were after your family. They started the fire that burnt your family's house down in Minnesota, and they're the ones responsible for the death of your parents."

Wren stared at her with wide eyes, not saying a single word or moving even an inch. He blinked a few times and shook his head. "Why?"

"He said something about united you guys were strong, with your combined abilities. They thought you were wasting your abilities by not joining their pack," she said.

Liya watched his eyes fill up with tears and she reached out her hand to him.

"I was right, all along. It *was* them," Wren whispered.

"What are you going to do, Wren?" Sutton suddenly asked and Wren and Liya glanced at him.

"We have to get Illa back first," Liya answered.

"Wren?" Sutton asked and raised his eyebrows.

"We have to get Illa back," Wren said as he looked at her. "Everything else will have to wait. I don't want to do anything risky."

"So, what *do* you want to do?" Liya asked. "Because I don't mind anything risky. You know I'd do anything to get Illa back."

"I know," Wren said with a tight smile and took Liya's hand.

"We'll get her back. Sutton, assemble the retrieval team. Luca, get Shea and her truck to my house as soon as she can."

"You're calling Shea again?" Luca asked and Wren gave him a look that was not to be contended with. Luca held his hands up in defense and nodded while he reached for his phone.

"What do I do?" Liya asked.

"You're coming with me," Wren said.

Liya followed Wren to his BMW, and they climbed inside. "Where are we going?"

"To my house," he answered.

"Why?" she asked.

"We need to pick up a few things. We're entering dangerous territory, so we'll need a few supplies," he answered vaguely and they spent the rest of the drive in silence.

Liya tried to figure out what Wren meant by supplies, but didn't ask him. She was too worried about Illa, and whether she was okay. She glanced over at Wren and noticed the blind hatred in his eyes and she knew that if he wasn't careful, he'd try to wipe out the entire Crescent pack.

Wren parked his car in the driveway, and they rushed into the house. Wren closed the door behind them, hurried down the hallway and opened a door on the right.

Liya had never noticed that door before and had always thought it was either the bathroom, or another bedroom. Wren stepped inside and switched on the light. Liya's jaw dropped as she gazed inside.

"What the hell..." she mouthed, gaping at the walls packed with multiple weapons, most of which she had never seen before in her life. Most of them looked old, and she asked, "Where did all these come from?"

"I retrieved them from my father's basement after the fire," he answered as he grabbed two crossbows from the wall.

"You went back there?" she asked and turned to him.

"Wouldn't you?" he asked, as if her question was the most ridiculous thing he had ever heard in his life.

She shrugged and wondered whether Wren was purely fueled by revenge at that very moment. Maybe she shouldn't have told him about what Hunter said to her because then he would solely focus on getting Illa back safely, but she didn't want to keep things from him anymore. He deserved to know.

"Wren?" she asked, and he looked at her as he took out a small box from a drawer in front of him.

"Yeah?" he asked expectantly.

"Look, I know you're upset about Hunter, and you might have a little more aggression inside you trying to claw its way out, and you might even be fueled by the thought of getting even with Hunter, but I..." She hesitated for a second. "I guess what I'm trying to say is that you don't need to go into full-rampage wolf mode."

"I'm not fueled by the need to get revenge on him, Liya," he said, but even though Liya nodded, she wasn't really convinced.

Ever since Wren had opened up to her about himself and his family, she discovered that he was very emotional, and in her experience, emotional often meant unpredictable in their actions, and feeling the need to right all the wrongs that had been done to them in their lives.

Liya remembered she referred to it as vigilante syndrome, where they sought out the guilty parties and made them pay for what they did.

"We're just getting Illa back, right?" she asked.

"Right," Wren said, loading the crossbow, "and if I happen to kill a bunch of Crescents in the process, then so be it."

"Wren..." Liya said with concern in her voice.

"Here," he said and held out a small box to her. "Put this on."

Liya took the box from him and looked inside. "You're giving me jewelry?" she asked, bewildered.

He grinned briefly and took the bracelet out of the box. "It's made of nickel and will mask any trace of your scent, which will make you virtually undetectable."

"Wow," she said and watched as he tied it around her wrist.

"Don't lose it. It was my mother's," he said, lingering for a second too long before turning away.

Liya gently fingered the links of the bracelet and smiled sadly. A part of her felt truly saddened by the way she and Wren were connected through Hunter, or perhaps sickened was the right word. The other part of her felt honored that Wren trusted her enough, and loved her enough for him to give his mother's bracelet to her. She desperately wanted him to pull her close to him and hold her, making all the pain and fear melt away. She wanted to feel the heat of his skin against hers and listen to his heart beating in his chest. She wanted him to tell her once again that he loved her and that he couldn't imagine a world without her and Illa in it. She wanted to feel wanted by him, and to say goodbye to the fear she had felt her entire life.

"Wren, could we just talk about—"

"No, Liya. Not right now," he said dismissively and shook his head. "Whatever we need to talk about can wait. Once we have Illa back home, then we can talk all you want. Okay?"

"Sure. That would be great," she said with a nod.

"This is for you," Wren said and handed her a fully loaded crossbow.

"For me?" she stuttered.

"Have you ever fired one before?" he asked and raised his eyebrows.

"No, but I can watch a quick tutorial online," she said mockingly.

Wren narrowed his eyes at her and shook his head. "Maybe you'd like something else. Maybe a machete?"

Liya reached out her hand and grabbed a machete that hung from the wall, and a strange feeling bubbled up inside her. She remembered her father taking her out into the fields when she was just a little girl, swinging machetes around in the farm fields. It had been such a long time ago, but Liya smiled confidently as she slid it off the wall, feeling the handle against her skin.

"I'll take both. I like the option of having both ranges on my targets, as well as being close enough to have their blood splatter on my face."

Wren froze and stared at her with wide eyes. His expression was a combination of surprise, awe, and absolute terror.

"What?" Liya asked as she swung the machete around with precise movements. "My dad showed me how not to kill myself with one of these when I was a little girl."

Wren smiled slightly and nodded. "You dad sounds great."

"He *is* great, and he raised an even greater daughter," she said and winked at him. "Can we go now?"

"Not dressed like that, babe," he said and motioned to her bottom half. "You wouldn't want to cover those cuddly sheep in wolf blood, would you?"

"Of course not. These are my favorite pants," she pouted, and he chuckled.

"Check the guestroom closet," he said and gestured to the door.

Liya didn't have to be asked twice, and quickly headed to the guest room closet. She opened the doors and a satisfied smile ran across her lips as she noticed the leather outfit inside. "This is definitely more like it."

She undressed quickly and slipped into the black leather pants, the dark green sweater, and the black boots. She loosened her hair, grabbed her crossbow and machete and met up with Wren, who was waiting for her in the kitchen.

He turned around and exhaled deeply. The corners of his mouth curled up and he nodded in approval.

"Wow," he whispered.

"Come on, baby. Let's go get our daughter back," she said to him and smacked her lips.

10

W ren inhaled calmly through his nose as he tried to figure out in which direction they needed to go. His BMW drove at a high speed along the motorway and the music blared from the radio. Even though he tried his hardest to keep himself focused, he occasionally glanced over at Liya, who looked unbelievably hot in her leather pants. Her blonde hair was loose and tousled and there was a certain kind of edge to her that he had never seen before.

When he first met her, she looked like a sweet young mother who was running away from her abusive ex-boyfriend. She still was, but now she was fueled by the same raw emotions as he was. The corners of his mouth curled up again as he noticed her foot tapping along to the song on the radio and he turned his attention back to the road as he adjusted the volume a little louder. Liya uncrossed her legs and licked her lips as she looked in his direction.

The heat rose in his body and he instinctively stepped on the gas pedal. They drove for a few miles before Wren caught a whiff of Hunter's scent and he eased his foot off the pedal.

Liya noticed it and turned the music down as she looked at him. "What is it?"

"He's changed direction."

"Where is he going?" she asked.

"East. Way east," Wren said, not sure if that was even right. "North Dakota, maybe?"

"Their Alpha doesn't live in North Dakota," Liya responded, and Wren stopped the car on the side of the road.

"Where *does* he live?" Wren asked.

"I have no idea. I haven't seen them since Illa was born. They just..." Her voice trailed off and she shrugged. "They just disappeared. I never heard Hunter say where."

"Do you think he's taking her to them?"

"I don't know."

"Wait, he's not stopping," Wren said.

"What do you mean? How can you tell?" Liya asked.

"Well, his scent would become stronger and clearer if he was stopping. We'd be closer to him, but he's still going."

"He still has her with him, right?" she asked, her eyes filling up with tears.

Wren bit his bottom lip and nodded.

"Then where the hell is he going?" she whispered.

Wren and Liya glanced at one another and Wren's eyes widened.

"What?" she asked, almost afraid to do so.

"I know where he's going," Wren said and shifted his car into first gear. "The bastard is taunting me."

"Wren, what are you talking about?" she asked.

"He's going back to Silver Bay, back to our old house."

"The house he helped burn down?" she asked, and he nodded. "Why?"

"Because he knows if I'm there, I won't be as strong. The memories are painful and that makes me weak."

Wolf's Baby 121

"You're going to listen to me right now, okay?" Liya said as she took his hand and he looked at her. "You're *not* weak. You're are strong and powerful, and don't you forget that. Ever. If you feel overwhelmed, I'm right here. I conceal those feelings of pain and regret for you," Liya said, and her blue eyes glowed in the twilight.

"No, I can't let you do that," Wren said and shook his head. Wren knew the intensity of his own memories and feelings, and if he allowed Liya to conceal them, she'd experience them as well. That was the last thing he wanted to do, because he knew how empty and fearful it left him, and he didn't want that for Liya.

"Your pain is my pain, right?" she whispered and squeezed his hand.

He nodded, knowing Liya was not going to take no for an answer. "Your pain is my pain," he repeated, and she nodded encouragingly at him.

Wren stepped on the gas pedal again and the BMW jetted off into the night.

"Wren," Liya said, breaking the silence, "I'm sorry I didn't tell you about Miles."

Wren's jaw clenched slightly and he shifted the gear lever into the next gear. "Why didn't you?"

"Well, as I said, I didn't feel ready to talk about him. It was hard for me when it happened, and it's still hard for me sometimes. Whenever I think about it, I get sick to my stomach, and..." Her voice trailed off. "I guess I was just afraid to talk about it with you because *we imprinted.*"

"I didn't know it was possible to imprint again," Wren said.

"If one dies, then it is possible. I think that Mother Nature doesn't want us to be alone, or something like that," she said.

"Did you love him?" Wren asked.

"I don't know how to answer that without hurting you," Liya

answered and glanced out the window.

"Anything but the truth will hurt me."

She straightened her spine and wrung her hands together. "I did. He was really sweet and wonderful."

"How old were you?"

"It was a few days after my three-hundred-and-eleventh birthday," she answered.

"Wow, that is a long time ago," Wren said simply.

"It was. My mother was convinced it was just puppy love," Liya smiled.

"How did he die?" Wren asked. "I know you said that a Crescent killed him, but how?"

When Liya took too long to answer, Wren briefly glanced over at her and said, "If you don't feel like talking about it, it's okay."

"No, I've been keeping this inside me for long enough. I deserve to put this to rest," she said with a smile. "We were taking a walk in the meadow behind his parents' house. It was a beautiful August morning, the sky was clear and blue, and there wasn't a cloud in the sky. I remember it like it was yesterday. I can still smell the wildflowers and the heat of the sun on my skin. My mother told me that I needed to come back home, but of course, I didn't listen. Miles and I walked along the stream, and three wolves approached us from out of the woods. We didn't know who they were, and we were quite surprised to see them, too. We lived in a small town where there weren't *that* many wolves around that we knew of. The wolves we *had* met were friendly, but not these three. They were hostile; they bared their teeth at us. Miles and I tried to talk to them, but they weren't interested in what we had to say. It was Miles who noticed the crescent-shaped medallions around their necks."

"They were all Gammas," Wren said suddenly.

"You know the Crescents really well," Liya said and glanced

at him.

"They killed my parents, and a whole lot of others, so I am kind of *obligated* to know," Wren said and looked briefly at her.

Liya took a deep breath. "They started to circle around us and two of them pounced onto Miles. I just heard his screams while the other wolf stared at me."

"They didn't hurt you?" Wren asked.

"They didn't even *touch* me," Liya said.

"That's strange. The Crescents are relentless and cruel. They don't usually spare anyone," Wren pointed out.

"I know."

"What if..." Wren's voice trailed off and he shook his head, the idea that lingered in his mind too ridiculous to repeat.

"What, Wren?"

"This is going to sound crazy—"

"As opposed to everything else that has been going on?" she asked.

"Good point," he muttered. "You know how there are Seers in a pack?"

Liya glanced at him and nodded.

"Well, I think that they know what's going to happen in the future, and they try to manipulate the present to bend the future into what they want it to be," Wren said.

Liya shook her head, saying, "You're right. It *does* sound crazy."

"Think about it. That wolf would have normally killed anything in its path, but it didn't, because you were too important to kill," Wren said and paused for a second as Liya processed his words. "Each one of my brothers, myself included, has an ability relating to the five senses. Kodiak had the sense of touch, or feeling, and could feel everything everyone else felt. Of course, he could easily switch it on or off whenever he wanted to."

"Dealing with other people's emotions seems like a curse more than a special ability," Liya cringed.

"It was. Kodiak suffered from terrible mood swings and headaches because of it," Wren answered. "Anyway, a few months before the fire, he encouraged me to teach myself to turn my sense of smell on and off at will. I didn't understand why exactly, but that night it came in handy. No one wants to smell their parents being burnt alive," Wren shuddered.

"That's just terrible," Liya cringed again, "and really graphic."

"Sorry," Wren said as he massaged his temples.

"So, you think Kodiak is a Seer, and he was trying to manipulate the present accordingly because he knew what would happen in the future?" she asked.

"Why else would he teach me how to reset my own dislocated shoulder," he asked, "when a few months down the line I'd have to do that exact same thing to myself?"

"I don't know, but this conversation is making me feel a bit unsettled," she said and shifted around in the seat.

"Same here," he said before an awkward silence filled the car.

Wren and Liya continued driving non-stop over the next twenty hours, following Hunter's scent. They didn't even stop to sleep, but just took turns driving.

Finally, Wren drove into Silver Bay and took the first left turn towards his old family home. Hunter and Illa's scent grew stronger with every second that they came closer and when the old, still-abandoned home finally came into view, standing in the darkness, an eerie feeling filled Wren to the core. He had not been back in Silver Bay for some time now, but it looked exactly the same as it had when he left. The gravel road that led to their house was still as bumpy as it had been, and he remembered the headaches Kodiak would get because of it.

The house towered out from behind the trees, and even though it was still just a shell of its former self, Wren could practically see himself and his brothers outdoors enjoying their large yard. A wave of nostalgia hit him hard and his mouth was set in a grim line as he parked the car on the unkept grass and switched it off.

A shiver ran down his spine as he opened the door and climbed out of the car, Liya doing the same, neither of them saying a word. Wren slowly made his way across the field, and as he glanced back, he noticed Liya grabbing her machete from the trunk of the car.

The door of the house suddenly creaked open and Liya's eyes widened.

As they stepped into the dark house, their eyes quickly adjusted to the darkness, and Wren tried to catch a whiff of Hunter's scent. It was coming from upstairs, and Wren's jaw clenched. He wasn't sure how sturdy the upper level of the house was, but as he stepped onto the first step of the wooden staircase, he was surprised that it was rock stable. Even though the house still looked the same way it had when he had last been here, the inside looked like it was in the beginning phases of a renovation. He glanced back at Liya, who was ready to slice something in half with her machete at a moment's notice, and he smiled slightly.

The floorboards creaked behind them, but when they whirled around, there was no one there.

They quietly went upstairs and split up in two different directions. The moonlight cast eerie shadows on the floor, which gave Wren the chills. He reached for the doorknob of the second door to the right, which used to open to his bedroom, but he paused. The memories of that night suddenly flashed before his eyes and he growled to himself, not wanting to allow it to have such an effect on him. He opened the door and stepped inside, but again, there was no one there. The window he had climbed out of, nearly dislocating his shoulder, was open, just like it had been that night, and he walked over to it. He gazed through the window at the backyard. The marsh was completely covered in snow, and he wasn't even sure if it was still there. He heard a thumping sound coming from the other room and he turned around. "Liya? Did you hear that?"

Footsteps came down the hallway and Wren's jaw clenched as he saw Hunter appear in the doorway.

"Welcome home, Wren," Hunter said with a wicked smirk.

"Where's Liya?"

"Oh, she's..." his voice trailed off and he glanced down the hallway, "...taking a nap, I suppose."

A deep growl escaped from Wren's throat and he almost instantly transformed into a wolf, his brown fur shining in the moonlight and his dark brown eyes filled with anger and hatred.

Hunter took a step back in surprise. "Wow, you are a big one, aren't you?" he snickered before he himself transformed.

Wren narrowed his eyes at the big black wolf standing in front of him, his blue eyes shining like sapphires in the darkness, and growled again. Wren lunged forward, grabbing Hunter by the neck, and the two wolves rolled around the hallway, biting and tearing at one another. Wren thought he had a pretty good handle on things, even when they broke through the balustrades and plummeted down to the ground floor. He had to admit that Hunter was pretty strong and a rather impressive fighter, but fighting was the one thing Wren was good at.

Wren heard a howl in the distance and for the split second that he glanced up, Hunter grabbed him by the throat and Wren

Wolf's Baby 127

felt his teeth sink into his skin. Wren barked angrily and threw Hunter off him. Hunter landed across the room and scrambled to his feet, baring his teeth at Wren.

Another howl was heard in the distance, and Wren immediately recognized it, howling loudly in return. Hunter flattened his ears before lowering his neck again, assuming his attack stance.

Wren heard a noise coming from upstairs, and in his moment of distraction, Hunter pounced on him, repeatedly biting him in the neck. The howling grew louder and the world seemed to spin around Wren. He eventually fell to the floor and watched as Hunter stepped away from him.

Hunter transformed back into a human and he wiped the blood from his mouth. "Not so strong now, are you, Alpha?"

Where's Illa, he silently screamed as he panted for air, trying to still the searing pain from Hunter's bites.

"Looks like you couldn't cut it as an Alpha, little Wren," Hunter snarled and took something from his pants pocket. Wren gazed up at Hunter as he walked out of the room and up the stairs.

Liya!

Within a few seconds, Hunter was back downstairs, no longer holding the small item in his hand. Hunter turned to Wren, who still didn't have the physical strength to get up off the floor, and crouched beside him.

"Thank you for making this much easier than I thought it would be, Wren. Really," Hunter said and casually walked out of the house, slamming the door behind him.

Wren smelled smoke coming from somewhere in the house and his eyes widened. He slowly pushed himself up onto all fours and howled weakly before he collapsed again on the floor. As the smoke filled the air, he was once again reminded of that night.

11

Liya pushed herself up from the floor and touched the back of her head. She wasn't sure how long she had been passed out, or what exactly had happened, but she gathered that she had been struck from behind by something hard, judging by the pulsating pain in her head. She glanced around her and noticed the smoke coming from one side of the hallway.

"Oh, shit," she muttered as she stood from the floor. She then realized that her machete was gone and her shoulders slumped. "Shit," she hissed through her teeth. She left the room and her eyes widened as she saw the flames licking their way up the hallway. Luckily, she noticed that the fire had started from upstairs and there was a clear path downstairs, but she had to find Wren. He could be in any of these rooms. She carefully made her way down the hallway, calling his name, but she didn't hear him answer. Every upstairs room was empty, and it was starting to heat up from the flames.

"Wren? Where are you?" she yelled as she ran down the hallway back to the staircase.

As she stepped down onto the first step, she saw Wren lying

on the ground below. She rushed downstairs, almost falling down herself, and slid up to him.

"Wren, are you okay? Can you hear me?" she asked desperately as she ran her fingers through his brown fur. She pressed her ear against his pelt and listened for a heartbeat. She let out a relieved breath when she heard a slow and weak heartbeat and she sat upright. A gasp escaped her throat when she saw the blood on the fur by his neck and she placed her hands on him. "Wren, please wake up," she begged as tears ran down her cheeks.

The door suddenly flew open, which startled Liya, but as she glanced over her shoulder, she felt a wave of relief. Sutton, Luca and Shea stood in the doorway, and Liya called out, "Luca, Wren is hurt."

Luca rushed over to them and felt for a pulse. "He's alive, but just barely."

"Can you help him?" Liya asked and Luca glanced at her.

"Of course," he said and placed his hands where the blood pooled in his fur. "It's just going to take a bit of time."

"We don't have time, Luca. Hunter is probably long gone with Illa," Liya scowled.

"We'll go find him," Shea said and Liya glanced at her with a surprised look on her face. Shea shifted her weight and lifted her head high. "Well? Don't you want to get your daughter back?"

"Of course, I just..." Liya's voice trailed off and she glanced at Sutton.

"Go. We'll catch up to you later," Sutton said.

Liya nodded, stood from the floor and walked toward Shea, who was already halfway out the door. Liya stepped outside and looked around her. "Where's your car?"

"Oh, we prefer the fresh air," Shea said in a confident tone.

Liya frowned and looked at Shea as they made their way

through the overgrown grass and Liya could understand how Wren and Shea could have ended up dating. Shea was tall, slender yet curvy and had long dark brown hair which sparkled in the moonlight, flowing like silk. She was curvy in all the right places and definitely had an abundance of sex appeal.

"Can I ask you a question?" Liya asked as she struggled to keep up with Shea's long steps.

"Sure, but if it's about why Wren and I broke up, I'm not at liberty to discuss it," Shea answered dismissively.

"Oh, okay. No, I just wanted to know why you're helping me find Illa," Liya said, not taking her eyes from Shea.

Shea stopped in her tracks and turned to Liya. "You're Wren's mate, and he's my Alpha. You're practically family."

"But you know nothing about me other than I'm Wren's mate," Liya said.

"You know nothing about me either, but you let me in your house," Shea said.

"That's different," Liya muttered.

"Look, we're wasting time, but if you must know, Wren and I weren't compatible. End of story. He saw you, he imprinted on you and now he's with you. No bad vibes, no hard feelings, so I suggest you get used to my company and get over it," Shea said. "*You* got the guy, so I don't know why you're still jealous."

Liya raised both hands in submission as Shea carried on walking. Shea was right. She had nothing to be jealous about. She was with Wren, or at least she thought she was.

Liya walked over to Shea, who now had a considerable lead, but eventually caught up to her. "I'm sorry. I didn't mean to come across as snide and bitchy towards you."

"That's okay," Shea answered. "You don't look like the type to be a bitch anyway. You're a nice girl, and that's why Wren likes you."

"Thanks," Liya said simply.

Shea stopped and looked at Liya. "Okay, are you ready?"

"Ready for what?"

Shea scoffed. She took a step back and Liya watched in amazement as Shea transformed. Liya had seen many transformations, but never one quite as easy and alluring as Shea's. It actually made her jealous for a moment, even though Shea told her she didn't need to be.

Shea, a pitch-black wolf with the brightest green eyes she had ever seen in her life, gazed at her expectantly. She cocked her head and transformed as well, although it was not quite as alluring as Shea. Liya shook her white fur as a chill ran through her wolf blood. Shea nudged her with her front paw, motioning to the woods, and Liya nodded.

The two wolves made their way through the wooded area, running faster than the wind. Liya hadn't felt this free in a very long time, and as she glided through the air, her paws barely touched the icy snow. Even though the wind was as cold as ice and the temperature was below freezing, her blood was hot and the driving force inside her gave her the energy to keep on running.

Illa, baby girl, Mommy's coming for you, she thought as she followed Shea through the mountains.

Liya noticed Shea's pace slow down and she let out a small yelp, motioning to the front. Liya raised her eyes and tilted her head to the side as her ears flattened against her head.

In front of them stood an old house, even creepier than the old Wylde house in Silver Bay, and Liya shivered. Beside her, Shea transformed into her human form, even more seductively than when she had transformed into a wolf, and Liya shook her head, also transforming.

"Don't thank me yet. We still have to get your little girl," Shea said. "Are you ready?"

"Of course," Liya answered.

"I like your confidence," Shea said with a smile.

The two women crept through the wooded area towards the house and hid in the shadows. They kept an eye on the house, and noticed movement coming from one of the windows. The room was dimly lit with what appeared to be a candle and Liya could hear two different people there, one of them being Hunter. The other's voice seemed familiar, but she couldn't place it.

"Okay, who do you want, Hunter, or the other guy?" Shea asked and looked at Liya. "Or is that a stupid question?"

"I'm going to rip that bastard apart."

"Just be careful that your rage and need for vengeance don't cloud your vision too much," Shea said.

"I won't."

"Okay, let's go, then. I'll keep the old guy occupied."

"The old guy?" Liya asked.

"Yeah, he looked like a much older version of Hunter," Shea said nonchalantly.

"Shea, wait. That's Hunter's grandfather," Liya said. "He's the Crescent Alpha."

Shea's eyebrows shot up and she pouted slightly. "Now *that* sounds like fun."

Before Liya could call her back, Shea disappeared into the darkness and Liya bit her bottom lip. She crept along the side of the house and found an open window. She quietly climbed through it and looked around her, trying to find anything that could possibly help her to incapacitate Hunter, but strangely enough, there was nothing in the room. She slowly opened the door and peeked out into the hallway. The room with the light on was at the other end, and she quietly made her way to the door. As she reached for the doorknob, she heard muffled voices in another room, and quickly opened the door. She stepped inside the room and closed the door quietly. Catching her

Wolf's Baby 133

breath and trying to calm herself down, as her heart was literally sitting in her throat, she turned around and saw a crib standing in the corner of the room. Her heart melted as she walked closer and saw Illa fast asleep and completely unaware of the entire situation she had been a part of. Illa probably still recognized her father's scent and thought she'd be safe with him.

Maybe she was. Maybe Liya was blowing this whole thing out of proportion. Maybe he just wanted to see his daughter and had to resort to drastic measures to do so when Liya burnt their house down and ran away with Illa in the middle of the night.

Liya knew exactly what was happening. She turned around and saw Hunter standing in the doorway. Not only was Hunter a tracker—a damn good one, as well—he was a master manipulator and had a way of making Liya look like the villain.

"Hunter," she said with an angry edge to her voice.

"I thought you were dead, love," he said and his old nickname for her—which she despised—made her cringe.

"I don't die that easily, Hunter," she gritted her teeth.

"Unlike our little Alpha boyfriend," Hunter chuckled. "Now *that* guy was easy to kill. You're better off, love. He was too weak for you."

"I didn't come here to talk, Hunter. I came to get Illa."

"You're not going to take her away from me again," Hunter said and crossed his arms. "Because if you try it again, you won't see the sun rise ever again."

"You're awfully cocky for someone who's about to get their ass kicked," Liya said.

Hunter laughed and shook his head. "You can't kick my ass even if you tried," he said, "but you're welcome to try."

Liya narrowed her eyes at him, watching him taunt her, raising his hands in the air and motioning to her to do her worst. "What are you waiting for, love? Come at me."

Hunter's words weren't even cold yet when Liya leapt

forwards and kicked him in the chest. He flew through the air, down the hallway, and landed on the wooden floor with a loud crash. He immediately leapt to his feet and rolled his shoulders.

"Wow, what the hell was that?" he asked as he dusted himself off.

"Don't worry. There's a whole lot more where that came from," Liya said and came at him again, throwing him down onto the ground. Her eyes glowed a fierce and relentless blue as she pressed the heel of her boot against his neck and growled. "I should just kill you right here and now."

"Do it," Hunter spat at her.

"For once in my life, I am not afraid of you anymore, Hunter. You might have thought that you had me under your thumb, but you don't. I am done with being your little doormat," she gritted her teeth.

As she pressed her heel harder against his throat, a sharp pain suddenly erupted in her shoulder and as she glanced back, she saw the older man, Hunter's equally psychotic and abusive grandfather, holding a crossbow. Liya exhaled slowly and looked at her shoulder, where one of the arrows of the crossbow was wedged into her skin.

Liya wasn't quite sure what exactly happened after that, but as soon as she fell to the ground gasping for air, the world started to spin around her. At one point, Shea entered the room, along with Sutton, Luca and Wren. There was a lot of fighting and through the blur of noise and color, she saw blood on the ground beside her. Wren kneeled at her side, yelling at Luca, or someone, but Liya couldn't hear anything. There was a loud ringing in her ears that blocked out all other sounds, and it was enough to make her want to rip her ears out. The pain from the arrow in her shoulder didn't ease, not even when the entire world faded away.

"Get Illa," were the last words she muttered before everything went black around her and she was pulled into the dark hole filled with regrets, pain and the empty feeling she had inside her where Hunter had ripped out her soul by taking her daughter away from her, and almost killing Wren.

HER SHOULDER WAS ON FIRE, but it was a slow burn, and it felt good. At least she could still feel something. She spun out from her unconscious state and instantly felt nauseated by the feeling of riding on a rollercoaster.

"She's awake," she heard a voice say and there was a scurry all around her.

Liya opened her eyes and sat up abruptly. She was on the couch in Wren's house, surrounded by Wren, Sutton, Shea, Luca and Krew, who was standing in the back with Illa.

"Illa," Liya gasped and held her arms out.

"Careful," Wren said, but she didn't listen to him. She stood from the couch and walked over to Krew.

Illa smiled happily and held her little arms out to her mother. Liya scooped her up in her arms and held her close to her. She breathed in the scent of her daughter and the ache in her heart subsided completely.

"I am so glad to have you back, baby girl," she whispered.

Liya felt a hand on her shoulder and she turned around. Wren stood in front of her, with a concerned but relieved look on his face. She smiled at him and he put his arms around her and Illa.

"What happened?" Liya asked.

"You don't remember?" Wren asked.

"Not really. I remember getting shot with a crossbow by Hunter's grandfather, but..." Her voice trailed off and her eyes widened. "What happened to Hunter, and his dad?"

"Well, Shea took care of his dad," Sutton said with a grin.

"Real good," Shea said with a grin. "I've got a thing for older men."

Liya cringed slightly and shook her head. "And Hunter?"

"We took care of him, Sutton and I," Wren said. "He won't be bothering you anymore, Liya."

"And he's all torn up about it, too," Luca said with a smirk.

Liya looked at him with a frown and asked, "You didn't, did you?"

Luca just shrugged and his nonchalance for performing such a vicious and violent deed gave her chills.

"You guys are..." Liya looked at Krew, then at Wren, and then the others, and smiled slightly.

"Wonderful?" Sutton asked.

"Invincible," Shea corrected him.

"Exceptional," Luca said with a confident smile.

"Irreplaceable," Wren said and placed his hand on Illa's head.

"Actually, I was going to say that you're my heroes," Liya said, "but all those apply as well."

Illa held her arms out to Krew and he took her from Liya.

"Looks like you've got a new job description, Krew," Wren said.

"With pleasure, Wren. With absolute pleasure," Krew smiled.

Shea stepped forward and turned to Wren. "Your new girlfriend is a total badass," she said with a smile.

"Thanks, you were pretty badass yourself," Liya said. "I still wanted to ask you, could you show me how to transform with such style?"

"A skill like that can't be taught, you know," Shea said as she put her hands in her pockets. "Besides, there's nothing wrong with your transformation process, although you *could* try not making such a racket."

"Old habits die hard. What can I say?" Liya replied and smiled at Wren. "Speaking of badass, there's something that I need you to help me with."

"And what's that?" Wren asked.

"You'll see," she said with a smile.

12

One Month Later

Wren paced around the small waiting room in a store he had never been to, not having any idea why he was there in the first place. Liya had dragged him there, but she didn't tell him anything at all. Wren didn't like it when he didn't know what was going on, especially not when it came to Liya.

After the whole thing with Hunter hunting her and Illa down, taking Wren back to his family home and the trauma he had suffered there, and almost dying, along with Liya almost dying as well, Wren had had enough action to last him an entire lifetime. Luckily, everything had returned to normal, and in a little twist, Liya and Shea became best friends. It didn't bother Wren as much, not even when the two girls started talking about him. He felt secure enough in his relationship with Liya to not give a damn what they were discussing.

Maybe a little, but only sometimes.

Wren *was* glad, however, that Liya fit in so well and so easily with the pack, and every single pack member adored her and

Illa. Krew gave up his Zeta status and became Liya's Beta, a position which had not been utilized for nearly five centuries.

The Crescents seemed to back off after Hunter was killed—ripped apart by Wren and Sutton—along with Hunter's father. It was a tremendous loss for the Crescents, but they realized that Wren and his pack were not to be messed with. With their best and only tracker killed a few months after they had already lost two other important members of their pack, the Crescents ran back to New Orleans, or so it seemed, until the dust settled.

They would be back, because that was what they did, but Wren and his pack would be ready. Ready to kill and destroy whatever threatened their peaceful existence.

The door suddenly opened and Liya stepped out into the waiting room with another woman who had a full arm tattoo, a piercing through her septum and short, bright purple hair.

"Hey, is everything okay?" Wren asked as he approached them.

"Oh, yeah. Liya was a superstar," the young woman said.

"Thank you, Cass," Liya said with a smile and hugged the purple-haired woman.

"You're welcome," Cass said with an equally wide smile and stepped away, retreating through the door.

"Who was that?" Wren asked.

"That was Cass. She's a tattoo artist," Liya answered simply.

"And why did you bring me to a tattoo artist?" Wren asked.

"I didn't bring *you* to a tattoo artist. I brought myself," she said and held her hand out to him.

He took it and immediately noticed the new tattoo on her hand. It was no longer scathed with the crescent moon, but now there was a red rose, with a small brown bird sitting on one of its petals and a drop of water on the other petal.

"The bird is a wren, which represents you, of course," Liya explained, "and the drop of water is—"

"Illa, because she's your calm from the storm," Wren said.

Liya smiled and nodded slowly. "Exactly. How did you know that?"

"You mumbled it while you were unconscious," Wren said.

"I did?" she asked, and Wren nodded. "Wow."

"Liya, that tattoo didn't make you one of them, you know," Wren said as he took her hand and ran his finger along the new tattoo.

"I know, but now it feels like they don't own me anymore, that I am my own person," Liya said with a smile as she glanced down at the red flower on her hand where the moon used to be. "Now, I'm free."

~

THE END

PREVIEW: FATED MATE

PREVIEW

Fated Mate
by Juniper Hart

Sometimes, when the winds settled, Nora would sit by the window in her studio and stare into the blinding snow, losing herself in the whiteness for hours. It seemed such a contrast to the dark images on her canvasses, the bloody reds and blacks melding together in a splotchy mess.

It was easy to do when Jerome was gone and she was left alone with no one but the house staff and her thoughts.

How many years have we lived in this forsaken place? she asked herself that morning, but she immediately dismissed the question, refusing to fall into the pit of despair threatening to consume her. She didn't know where this melancholy had come from—she only knew that it was slowly starting to pile atop her shoulders.

The more Nora thought about it, the less she was able to remember a time before their escape to the alps. Though the fact depressed her greatly, there was no one she could speak to about it; no one but the white canvasses around her, which turned black with her innermost thoughts.

Sighing, she turned away from the endless falling snow and gazed at her supplies, wondering if she would get any work done soon.

It is not as if anyone is waiting on me, Nora thought with some bitterness.

It had been quite a long time since a deadline had created a light of excitement in her soul. Gone were the days of agents and accounts. Then again, there had never truly been any people waiting to purchase one of her pieces.

Now, instead of the promise of business, all that remained was the icy, but beautiful, Swiss days and the long, starlit nights where she pined for a different time.

I can't stay here, she thought mournfully. *I will lose my mind.*

Slowly, Nora rose from the cushioned window seat and reluctantly headed toward the door, her silk nightgown swirling around about her slender ankles as she moved. Tentatively, she opened the door and peered into the corridor before slipping out into the brightly lit house.

"Ah, *mademoiselle!*"

Nora froze in her tracks, slowly turning to address the woman who had called out to her: Collette, the housekeeper.

"Are you hungry?" she asked, smiling kindly. "I will fix you some breakfast, if you'd like."

"No, thank you," Nora said, immediately shaking her head.

Collette's green eyes narrowed, and Nora could tell she was about to be lectured.

"*Mademoiselle* Nora," she began, "you have not eaten properly in days. I realize that *artistes* are a different breed of person, but you are still a person, are you not? You must eat something!

Monsieur Charpentier will be displeased when he calls for your update and I tell him you have not touched a morsel of food."

Nora bit back a scathing remark and lowered her dark eyes toward the Calamander wood of the floor beneath her bare feet.

If Jerome has such concerns, he can deal with me himself, she thought to herself, but of course, she said nothing to Collette. It was not the housekeeper's fault that she had been named babysitter to Nora while Jerome was gone. Why did she even require a babysitter in his absence? Was there something wrong with her? Did Jerome not trust her to be alone?

"I will fix you whatever you please, *chérie,*" Collette continued, eyeing her pleadingly, and Nora stifled a sigh. It wouldn't do either of them any good, and she didn't want to get Collette in trouble.

"Whatever you want, Collette," she replied dully. "I just want to shower and change first."

The older woman's face exploded into a look of relief so great that Nora felt guilty for having been locked up in her room.

I am not the only one who is trapped under the thumb of that unbending brute, she thought, but she was again consumed with shame. Jerome loved her, and he only wanted what was best for her. *How dare you think of him so rudely? You are lucky no one can hear your thoughts.*

"What shall I have waiting for you, *mademoiselle?*" Collette pressed as Nora turned to leave.

Nora sighed to herself. "I... I will decide as I bathe."

There was never enough quietness for her to get some peace of mind—not unless she sat inside her studio and lost herself in the snow globe of her life, disconnected from the rest of the household.

She ascended the floating staircase to the second floor of the chalet, vaguely aware of the skylights emanating weak, gray rays onto the pristine interior of the place she had called home.

Living in the alps had been Jerome's idea all those years ago, and Nora tried to recall the excitement she experienced when he had first suggested it.

"Just imagine, *chérie*," he had said, his blue eye glimmering with the prospect. "You and me in our own paradise, separated from the scandal of the rest of the world. No judgements, no distractions. Only each other and our art. We can finally live the life we have always dreamed about."

It had been appealing, and it had been truly wonderful at first, but then his work had abruptly consumed his life, and suddenly, it was only Nora and her art rather than the two of them and *their* art.

Why does he leave me for such long periods? It was not a fair question to ask herself. Although Nora knew that Jerome didn't have any other choice, she couldn't help feeling resentful of him, despite being fully aware that, if she were in his shoes, she would do the exact same thing. If she were given a chance to leave this glass prison and meet with the outside world again, of course she would take it.

A pang of sadness filled her heart as she entered the master bedroom, slipping her nightgown over her head. Tossing the delicate item aside, she made her way into the spacious dressing room, another skylight illuminating the otherwise dim room.

Nora wanted to know what time it was, and she glanced around for a clock before remembering that, for being such a splendid home, there were so few clocks in the house.

Jerome preferred it that way.

"It is so much better without the constraints of time hanging over our heads, don't you agree, *chérie*?" he often said, and Nora agreed with him, just like she always did.

Day and night were only marked by darkness and light, the hours losing their purpose as she grew more and more reclusive.

I still have my art, she told herself as she gazed at her naked frame in the mirror. *If nothing else, I must remember I still have my art.*

Jerome had once described her as ageless, a timeless beauty of classical proportions with the porcelain skin of a doll and the even features of a Madonna. A tangled mop of ebony hair spilled indifferently along her shoulders, almost touching her slender waist in a mass of unkempt waves.

Nora put her hands up to examine her reflection, fingertips tracing the lines of her full lips and high cheekbones. She leaned forward, studying the deep brown of her irises as though she could stare into her own soul.

Are you still in there? she asked herself. *Am I still in there?*

A noise in the bedroom caused her to whirl, and she gazed out into the master bedroom to see Alex tidying the chambers, oblivious to her naked employer watching.

Alex used the feather duster to work along the expensive furnishings, humming softly to herself as music apparently piped into her ears through her earbuds.

Nora stepped back into the shadows of the dressing room, but she continued to watch the girl do her work. For a moment, Nora envied her. What she wouldn't give to be a chambermaid again, emptying chamber pots and living her life as a free woman without the pain she had now.

Nora shook her head to herself. Where had that thought come from? She had never in her life been a chambermaid.

I was born into a rich family like a princess who found her handsome prince, she laughed to herself. *A prince who swept me away to live in an ice palace.*

"*Mademoiselle* Nora!"

She jumped at the startled cry from Alex when she finally

noticed she had been watching her work. Nora forced a smile onto her face and showed herself before the young girl, who gaped at her in horror.

"I did not know you were here! Forgive me!" Alex continued, backing away, but Nora shook her head, her hair bobbing around her.

"I am glad you are here," she said. "You can brush my hair before I bathe."

Alex popped her earbuds out, her face stained with an embarrassed pink flush.

"Of course, *mademoiselle*," the maid replied, darting her eyes downward. "I'll find you a robe."

Nora waved her hand dismissively.

"There is no need," she told Alex. "I will shower directly after."

Alex swallowed visibly, but she did not argue as Nora moved toward her before plopping down in the chair facing the vanity. Alex reached for a hair brush so that she could begin.

"How are you liking it here, Alex?" Nora asked as the girl gently tried to make sense of the mess that was her hair.

As Nora looked at her reflection, she wondered when was the last time she had brushed her hair? Had she truly wasted away so much time? So many days?

"Very much, *mademoiselle*," Alex quickly answered. "Everyone is so nice here."

A small smile formed on Nora's lips. "Yes," she agreed. "The staff is well screened. Jerome and I have little patience for drama, you see."

Alex did not respond, but Nora thought she saw a glint of worry in the girl's face. What did Alex know about her and Jerome? Well, whatever it was, it didn't matter, not really.

If Alex did her job and kept her mouth shut, she had little to worry about. If she did not, she would be replaced as the ones before her had been.

At least that was Jerome's mentality.

Nora was more apprehensive about what the staff learned about her, as little information as it could be.

"I don't know why you care so much," Jerome had sighed once. "What can they possibly do?"

He does not have as much to lose as I do, Nora reminded herself. *What if my parents come to look for me, even after all these years?*

"And are you finding your accommodations comfortable?" she asked Alex instead. "Have you enough room? Everything you need?"

"Yes, *mademoiselle*," Alex replied, and although her voice wasn't all that convincing, Nora could not tell whether she was being sincere.

I have been out of touch with people too long, she thought. *Do I really not know how to tell when someone is lying to me?*

She turned to eye the blonde maid over her shoulder.

"You do not find it too isolated here?" Nora asked.

Alex's mouth parted slightly, as if she were searching for the right words to answer her question.

"It is much farther away from Lucerne than my previous employer," Alex agreed. "But Collette has a car arranged to take us to the city on our off days."

Nora nodded. "As it should be. You will find that *Monsieur* Charpentier and I can be quite flexible. We only expect that you show us loyalty, and we will do the same."

"Yes, *Mademoiselle* Nora."

"You may call me Nora," Nora explained, stifling a sigh at the girl's words. She winced slightly as Alex tugged slightly too hard against her head.

"*Oui, mademoiselle,*" Alex replied, and Nora tried not to roll her dark eyes skyward.

It was a losing battle when Jerome ran the show. The staff would never call her by her first name. It 'bred familiarity,' according to the all-knowing Jerome.

"And we all know that familiarity breeds contempt," he had added.

"Yet you continue to stay with me," Nora had reminded him, earning a chuckle from him.

"We are bound together," he had told her, "whether or not we like it."

Something about his words had filled Nora with sadness. What kind of life was this for either of them? Why should they hide themselves from the rest of the world?

"Have I said something wrong, *Mademoiselle* Nora?" Alex questioned as she noticed the sudden look on her face. She had finished brushing Nora's head, so Nora shook her head in response.

"No, Alex," she replied. "I am going to shower. Please tell Collette that I will have toast and grapefruit with coffee afterwards."

"Yes, *mademoiselle*. Right away," Alex breathed. She seemed immensely relieved to be dismissed, and she hurried toward the doorway as if she was worried Nora would change her mind.

Nora watched her leave, her heart sinking slightly. She couldn't even pay the young girl to sit there with her, though she didn't know why she was surprised. It didn't matter how much she and Jerome tried to keep their secrets under wraps—someone would always learn the truth.

As if we are freaks who do not deserve to live in society, Nora thought angrily. *That is why Jerome moved us out this way. To remove us from public scrutiny.*

Despite the fact that this was not a new understanding—despite the fact that she already knew this—it still filled her with longing.

Times were changing. There was no reason for them to hide who they were from everyone else.

Of course, Nora was not so naïve. She knew that no matter how much the world had progressed, there were certain aspects that would always remain the same.

Stop your wallowing, she chided herself crossly. *Have a shower and have something to eat. Then you can return to the studio and do some work.*

With new resolve, Nora rose from the vanity and wandered back through the dressing room and into the bathroom. Looking around at the steam shower and clawfoot bathtub, she reminded herself that she had everything she could ever want. She sighed, leaning forward to run the water, annoyed at her own dark mood.

You have an artist's temperament, she thought wryly. *If you are going to feel sorry for yourself, at least put it into your artwork.*

But it was easier said than done.

Nora dipped herself into the rose-scented water and allowed the warmth to sweep over her body. As much as she had hoped it would be, this was no instants solution to her mood. How could there be when she had never gotten what she wanted out of life?

She groaned aloud.

"What is wrong with me today?" she growled to herself, and she wondered if maybe she was getting cabin fever.

Nora tried to remember the last time she had left the sprawling cottage for any reason. It had been months, she was sure, and the realization made her sit up in the tub, her eyes widening in disbelief.

I have completely lost touch with reality, she thought, rising from the bath even though she had not bothered to soap or wash her hair.

"Alex!" she yelled. "Collette!"

A moment later, both women appeared in the doorframe of the bathroom, their faces etched in worry.

"Yes, *mademoiselle*?" they chorused. "Are you all right?"

Nora nodded.

"Have Marc warm up the car," she said. "We're going to Lucerne."

Collette stared at her as if she had sprouted another head.

"*Mademoiselle*?" she choked. "You are going to town alone?"

Nora chuckled. "No, we're all going to town. Get dressed."

Collette and Alex exchanged a long look.

"Is something wrong?" Collette asked again. "Should I call for *Monsieur* Charpentier? Shall I have Marc go and get you something you need?"

Nora snorted as Alex quickly handed her a towel, casting her eyes aside.

"Not everything needs to go through Jerome," she sighed. "This is my house, too. If I wish to visit town, I do not see the need for it to be a production."

"*Bien sûr*," Collette replied quickly, her face blushing crimson. "I only meant—"

"I know what you meant," Nora interjected. She couldn't blame Collette; after all, her job included reporting back to Jerome and keeping him updated. "And Jerome doesn't have a say in a girls' afternoon."

Once again, Collette and Alex looked at each other. "Girls' afternoon?"

"Yes," Nora told them. "Get your things. We're going for lunch and shopping."

Their mouths fell open in unison, but to Nora's relief, they did not argue any further. Instead, they turned to leave the bathroom, almost tripping over one another.

Nora wrapped the thick towel around her svelte frame and gazed at herself in the steamy mirror.

Lunch, shopping, and gossiping should cure my mood, she thought, wiping the haze from the glass. *I will find something sexy to wear for Jerome when he finally comes home. That will surely cure my melancholy.*

To continue reading Fated Mate, download the Misty Woods Dragons Shifter Romance Collection on Amazon.

OTHER BOOKS YOU WILL LOVE

Birch Mountain Alphas
Dark Secrets, sexy romantic encounters, and alpha shifters who know how to take charge. This shifter box set is sizzling hot, and ready to be devoured!

Element Dragons Box Set
Four powerful dragon princes are in pursuit of their lifelong mates.

Misty Woods Dragons: Shifter Romance Collection
Six dragon princes and more in a hot shifter romance collection.

SECRET WOODS BOOKS

Receive a FREE paranormal romance eBook by visiting our website and signing up for our mailing list:

SecretWoodsBooks.com

By signing up for our mailing list, you'll receive a FREE paranormal romance eBook. The newsletter will also provide information on upcoming books and special offers.

THANK YOU

Thank you for reading my book. Readers like you make an author's world shine. If you've enjoyed this book, or any other books by Lola Gabriel or another author, please don't hesitate to review them on Amazon or Goodreads.

Every single review makes an incredible difference. The reason for this is simple: other readers trust reviews more than professional endorsements. For this reason, indie authors rely on our readers to spread the good word.

Thank you very much! I am giving you a virtual high-five!

Lola Gabriel

ABOUT THE AUTHOR

Lola Gabriel loves reading and writing paranormal romances. Growing up in the Pacific Northwest, she has fond memories of retreating to the woods for long hikes. The towering evergreens, natural waterfalls, and soothing rain often set the scenery for her characters' romantic encounters.

Find out more about Lola Gabriel at SecretWoodsBooks.com

Made in the USA
Lexington, KY
04 May 2019